CRITICS LOVE
GLORIA WHITE'S TWO PREVIOUS
RONNIE VENTANA MYSTERIES

CHARGED WITH GUILT

"Gloria White's crackling new Ronnie Ventana
mystery gets off to a fast start. . . . White keeps
us guessing . . . [and] keeps the pages turning."
—*San Francisco Sunday Examiner & Chronicle*

"TAUT, TENSE, TOUCHING, AND EXCITING, *Charged
with Guilt* charges to the top of the hard-boiled
heap. Buy it, read it—you won't put it down."
—Joe Gores, author of *Menaced Assassin*

"The plot of *Charged with Guilt* twists and turns
with more surprises than a nighttime tour of the
City by the Bay."
—*Mostly Murder*

MONEY TO BURN

"WHITE AT HER BEST: fast-paced and tightly written
. . . a likable and down-to-earth character."
—*San Francisco Chronicle*

"A FAST-PACED ADVENTURE . . . a web of personal
relationships and professional intrigues that
reach into surprising crannies."
—*Publishers Weekly*

"A likable new detective. . . . Ventana is complex
and charming."
—*Cape Cod Times*

Also by Gloria White

CHARGED WITH GUILT
MONEY TO BURN
MURDER ON THE RUN

SUNSET
AND
SANTIAGO

GLORIA WHITE

A DELL BOOK

Published by
Dell Publishing
a division of
Bantam Doubleday Dell Publishing Group, Inc.
1540 Broadway
New York, New York 10036

The trademark Dell® is registered in the U.S. Patent and Trademark Office.

ISBN: 0-440-22326-1

Printed in the United States of America

Published simultaneously in Canada

February 1997

OPM   10   9   8   7   6   5   4   3   2   1

In memory of
GASTÓN GUILLEMARD

Alma alegre
Corazón valiente

1

ou can never own the night in San Francisco, but sometimes, in the cold hours before dawn, the city can reach out and take hold of your soul. It was two A.M. the morning of April 24, and the city had my heart firmly in its grasp.

A big drop of moisture fell onto the outdoor bench where I sat. It fell like doomsday from the thick branches of eucalyptus above me. I peered upward into the thick fog, then back at the electrical pole gleaming through the mist from the concrete median down the center of Sunset Boulevard. And I tried again for the millionth time to imagine how it must have happened.

The car hadn't skidded far. The black tire marks on the pavement had stretched only fifteen feet, dark slashes against the lighter gray. Then the median curb, the scorch marks. And the pole. The pole that had stood fast and strong twenty years ago against the fatal impact of the speeding car.

It had been awful to see that mangled pole

for the first time, scarred and burned like the small patch of grass around it, like the pavement beyond, like I imagined my parents had been. I remember thinking how violent and stupid that pole looked, like a brute animal without a brain.

And when I touched it twenty years ago, on that horrible night, my hand came away black. And when I struck it, over and over again with my fist, it hurt me, too, like it had my parents. I'd worn a cast on my hand for weeks afterward, until the small bones of my palm healed, and every time I looked at the stark, white plaster wrapped around my hand, I ached to bring them back.

I hated that post for the longest time. Then, one year, sitting on the bench, keeping my anniversary-night vigil, I realized that the post— the electric light pole that had mangled my parents' car and had stood fast while it smashed the life and soul out of their fragile bodies—that that post had somehow become, if not my friend, at least the one constant in my life.

The cold damp sank into my bones as I stood and crossed the deserted boulevard in the dark. I reached out and laid my palm gently against the roughened gray surface of the post. It was as cold and dead and dumb as it had been that morning twenty years ago. Twenty years ago today. But now, this time, when I lifted my hand it came away clean.

2

I was still sitting out there on the bench on Sunset when they drove up. That's why I didn't notice them at first. I was pretty much lost in my own thoughts, thinking about the accident, thinking about how much that single fraction of time had so changed my life, and about the fact that it had happened right here twenty years ago. Twenty years ago to the hour.

I was all wrapped up remembering, so when I heard the car pull up in the dark behind me, it didn't really register. After all, I couldn't see them, and they probably couldn't see me. But when they started talking above the soft purr of the idling engine, their low, agitated voices traveled easily through the fog.

". . . the leg," one voice said. "*¡Coño, idiota!* Get the leg!"

"*No seas pendejo.* I got it. No—*¡espera!* It's stuck."

"I *know* it's stuck, *imbécil*. Get it loose."

"Fucker didn't look this heavy."

"Just roll him out, *pendejo*. Do it."

I heard the rustle of shrubs and maybe a *thunk*—but I could have imagined that. Then, before I could even think of moving or calling out, I heard a soft *swish-swish-swish*—the unmistakable sound a synthetic windbreaker makes when you move—then the slap of hurried feet on pavement, the roar of an engine accelerating, and two car doors slamming shut.

It all happened so fast, I could have dreamed it. The sound of the car was quickly fading, but I jumped up and ran across the grass lawn toward it, toward Thirty-seventh.

"Hey!" I shouted. "Hey, you!"

On a clear night I could have made out the license number, but in tonight's fog all I saw was a shrinking dark hulk in the distance and receding taillights sparkling dimly at me through the mist. And then they were gone.

In the sudden quiet the darkness seemed to close in around me. I found myself on the damp sidewalk uneasily scanning the grassy patch I'd just crossed. They had dumped something. Something heavy. Something with legs.

The light from the streetlamp wasn't as strong here as it was over at the bench where I'd been sitting. I couldn't see much.

Shrubs. They'd been rustling through the shrubs. I walked carefully toward a stand of bushes and looked around, squinting into the darkness. Nothing.

Farther in, closer to the bench, closer to

Sunset, was another clump of shadows. I started toward it, then noticed a big lump—something dark and still—on the grass a few feet away.

I took a deep breath, then started across the wet grass. My feet sank into moist earth as I moved forward, keeping my eyes focused on the lump in case it moved. I was about ten feet away when my limbs froze. All of a sudden the cold night air snatched my breath away and my heart seemed to stop. It—he—the lump—was a man crumpled on his side in a fetal position. He lay still and silent on the soft wet ground.

In the dim light his clothes looked casual—a light corduroy sport jacket over jeans and loafers—and he seemed to be around my age—thirty-four—and handsome in a nerdy, bookish kind of way. I stepped in closer.

"Hey," I said softly. "Hey, mister. Are you all right?" Then louder. "Can you hear me?"

Nothing. He lay still as death on the ground.

I took a few more steps and bent over him, wondering if it would be easier to find a pulse in his wrist or in his neck. The neck, I decided.

Okay. One last deep breath. I dropped to one knee beside him and sort of poked his shoulder. "Hey, mister."

My own heart was beating so fast I could hardly breathe. I prodded him again, then pinched the corduroy of his jacket between my fingers and pulled. "Hey!" I said. "Wake up!"

He sort of slumped when I let go of his sleeve and he rolled over, facedown in the grass.

"Shit." I braced my legs and grabbed his

shoulder, then flipped him over faceup. He felt like lead, but I thought I heard him groan when his head lolled onto the wet grass.

I stared at his face, fascinated. He looked like a studious kind of guy, pale skin, blondish hair trimmed short, and a square chin but with the scrawny kind of body of somebody who doesn't exercise much. He didn't look like somebody who'd get into this kind of trouble.

"Hey!" I shook him again. "You okay? Wake up!"

Nothing.

I laid two fingers gently under his jawline where I figured his jugular might be. The skin of his neck felt warm—a good sign—and a faint waft of alcohol hit my nostrils.

"Be alive," I whispered, pressing harder against his neck. His handsome face looked serene. His eyes were closed. His skin was ashen, but that could have been because of the poor lighting. He didn't look damaged, and as far as I could tell, he wasn't bleeding. But something was definitely wrong.

I tore off my jacket and threw it across his chest, then sprinted across the street and started pounding on doors.

"Help! Help! Call 911," I kept shouting.

And finally somebody did.

2

The guys with the ambulance showed up first. Then came the fire truck and then, later, the cops and the coroner's staff and a whole team of Homicide backup people to comb every inch of ground between where the guy was dumped and Thirty-seventh Avenue. After the first five minutes nobody seemed to think things were too urgent anymore, so that pretty much confirmed my hunch that the poor guy was dead.

"I don't know him," I said to what seemed like the tenth guy who asked.

I kept waiting for Philly Post to show up, but all I got was a rough version of Tweedledum and Tweedledee—two chubby guys who'd probably lose their pensions if they ever had to pass the physical-agility test again. Their names were Checker and Marks, but I couldn't remember which was which. One of them told me he thought Post was on vacation.

They kept circling the area like two bloated

buzzards looking for more dead bodies to put them over the top. After things had sort of settled down from the initial frenzy, one of them swept by me. I was behind the yellow police tape, but nobody was watching, so I slipped inside again and caught up with him.

I took a guess. "Officer Marks?"

He didn't stop.

"Officer Checker?"

The fat guy pulled up and turned around, moving with all the deliberate speed of a river barge. He blinked his eyes at me like he'd just come off a three-day drunk. "Huh?"

Great. The guy had broccoli for brains. Either that or he was still half asleep. I smiled, but he didn't smile back.

"I was wondering," I began. "Who's the dead guy? Did he have any identification?"

Tweedle stared at me like I was a poodle talking Latin. He glanced at the string of yellow tape behind me, then gave my face a steady second look to make sure I wasn't somebody he knew. "You supposed to be in here?"

"I'm the person who called the ambulance. I'm the witness."

"Oh, right." He looked around at all the activity and seemed pleased there was so much going on.

"So who is he?" I asked.

"Maybe we better walk over here." Tweedle beckoned for me to follow and river-barged his way back toward the yellow tape.

"Look," he said when we reached it. "My partner says this guy was a friend of yours."

"Why would I be asking you who he is if he was a friend of mine?"

He took a few seconds to absorb that. "Are you saying you don't know him?"

"I've never seen him before in my life."

"You sure? Hah! Listen to what I'm saying! Of course, you're sure. You didn't know the guy, you didn't know him. Okay, why don't we sit down and talk about this?"

Checker grunted as he bent to pass under the yellow tape, then once on the other side, he led me over to an unmarked brown car and opened the front passenger door.

"Have a seat," he said, then ambled around the front of the car to the driver's side.

Inside, the whole car reeked of fried food. No mystery about what had happened to these guys' waistlines.

Checker wedged himself and his stomach in behind the steering wheel. He looked uncomfortable as hell.

"So what happened?" he asked, producing a tiny notebook from nowhere and reaching for a pen on the dash.

I explained how I'd been sitting on the bench when somebody dumped the body on the grassy patch behind me, how I'd tried to revive him, and how I'd finally gotten some good but sleepy citizen to open his door and phone 911. Checker nodded and grunted a few times, but never once touched pen to paper. Maybe he was smarter than he seemed. Or maybe he was as stupid as he looked.

He turned his bulging eyes on me and regarded me with what I think he considered his don't-try-to-fool-me-missy look. "So what are you doing out here at two in the morning?"

Since before the ambulance had arrived, I'd been trying to think of some explanation besides the truth. I'd come up blank.

"There was a car wreck here twenty years ago," I began. My voice sounded flat. "My parents died. I—uh—I usually—Once a year I usually come out here and sit for a while."

"Yeah?" Checker looked skeptical.

I didn't say anything.

"Twenty years ago, huh?" He glanced at his watch. "April twenty-fourth the anniversary?"

I nodded and braced myself when he suddenly slapped his thigh, pointed a finger at me, and grinned. "It was a car wreck, right?"

I didn't say yes and I didn't say no, but Officer Checker kept on grinning.

"You're talking about the Ventana cat burglars, aren't you? I saw that in the paper a couple of years back. You're the daughter. You come out here every year, two o'clock. Yeah. I saw the write-up."

He sat there a few seconds nodding, I guess congratulating himself for his great deductive powers, maybe thinking he was Sherlock Holmes. Then he said, "They buried nearby?"

"What's that got to do with the dead guy over there on the grass?"

"Well . . ." He frowned and rubbed the back of his fat neck like I'd seen wily old detectives do on TV a million times. "Wouldn't it make more sense just to go over to the cemetery? I mean, I'm only suggesting it because if that's where they're buried, you could do it in the daylight."

I took a deep breath and told myself getting angry with him would be like getting angry at a farm animal for not having social skills. "It's what I do, Officer Checker. It makes sense to me."

He nodded, then surprised me by apologizing and getting all misty-eyed.

"You know, your folks . . . You think they're always gonna be around," he said. "I lost both of mine too. Just last year. Ma had a stroke and was gone in minutes. Three months later the old man tells me he's got liver disease. He never saw the Fourth of July." He glanced over at me and his face had turned to mush. "Must have been rough on you. I mean, I'm going on forty-three this year and it hurt like hell to see 'em pass on. You musta been just a kid."

"Was this guy dead when they dumped him out there?" I asked.

Checker cleared his throat and hesitated.

"I just want to know if there was anything I could have done for him," I said.

"Nothing." He glanced out the window and watched two men lift the dead guy into a body bag. "M.E. thinks it was a blunt instrument to the back of the head. Thinks he died instantly. Won't know for sure until he works it, though. You told me you knew him?"

"I said I *didn't* know him."

"Oh, yeah. That's right."

"Who is he? What's his name?" He'd looked so innocuous. I couldn't imagine why anybody would want to kill him.

"Won't know until we run the prints."

"Doesn't he have a driver's license or some kind of I.D.?"

"They cleaned him out. But even if he did have an I.D., we wouldn't get a confirm until we run prints." He glanced down at the blank page of his notebook. "So did you see the guys that dumped him? Car? Make? Model?"

I thought I'd been totally focused on dealing with the dead guy, but now that I thought about it, I remembered that the shadow I'd seen moving down the street had seemed dark and large. It could have been a van. I told Checker as much, then shook my head when he pressed me further.

"I really didn't see anything. I heard two voices. They said some words in Spanish, but mostly they talked in English about getting the guy out of the car. And that's about it."

A knock on Checker's window startled us both. It was Marks. He was holding something in his raised hand and talking. Checker rolled down the window.

"This yours?" Marks asked.

I looked closer, then nodded. It was my jacket, the one I'd thrown over the guy to keep him warm while I waited for the police to show.

Marks handed the jacket to somebody behind him, then turned back to me. "We're gonna keep it for evidence. You can have it after the lab's done with it. You say this guy was a buddy of yours?"

I looked at my watch. It was almost three o'clock. I'd spent what felt like the last twenty minutes listening to Checker moan about his dead parents and grill me about mine. I wasn't in the mood to repeat everything I'd already said all over again.

I thought about telling him to ask Checker, but Checker was watching me like he was dying to hear my answer, like he hadn't heard me tell him five minutes ago that I'd never seen the guy in my life. I sighed.

"No, Officer," I said. "I never met him."

4

was so tired that when I turned the steering wheel of my trusty blue Toyota to make the corner onto Grant Avenue, my arms felt like lead. It was just past ten o'clock in the morning. And I'd spent the past two hours down at the Hall of Justice with Checker and Marks "cooperating" and intermittently daydreaming about the warmth of my lumpy sofa bed.

By the time I hit North Beach, I was fighting to keep my eyelids up. Then I saw a rangy kid pacing up and down in front of my apartment building and I had to smile.

She was an androgynous fourteen-year-old, flat-chested and lanky in fashionably faded baggy clothes, dark-skinned, with wavy, overdue-for-a-wash dark hair. Her eyelids were caked with enough iridescent green eye shadow to last anybody else three decades.

"Hey!" I said, after I'd parked the car and come around the corner.

She looked up, startled, wary. Then her solemn eyes lit up and she grinned.

Up close she was a mess. The glittery green eye shadow was smeared, her lips were pale, and she had big dark circles under her eyes. Her clothes looked slept in. But she was excited— excited and maybe a little scared.

"What's going on, Marina?" I forced myself to be casual. Since she'd helped me on my first big murder case a year ago—a case that ended up freeing her from an abusive uncle—we'd kept in touch, mostly going for hikes in the redwoods and eating the occasional pizza. Her parents were dead, her aunt was spineless, and her friends were borderline barrio gangstas. The way I saw it, I was the only semipositive role model she had. "You off from school today?"

She rolled her eyes. "School? I'm supposed to go to school when junk like this is going down?"

"Junk like what?"

She hesitated. "Promise you won't get mad?"

I looked her up and down. She seemed to be all in one piece—no visible bruises, no dried blood. She just looked tired. "You're not hurt, are you?"

She fingered the strap of her black leather backpack and gave me a queer look. "Nuh-uh."

"Okay. Then I won't get mad."

"Promise?"

"Are you going to tell me or not?"

"I just don't want you to get mad, that's all. Will you promise?"

"I already have, Marina." I glanced down the

street. "When you get ready to talk, I'll be over there having breakfast."

Café Rossini's quiet and I've got a deal with the owners, where I get free espresso for six months because I wired their back door for them after a break-in.

Marina followed me inside and ordered a croissant, two muffins, a piece of cake, and hot chocolate. She seemed surprised when all I asked for was a cappucino.

"Okay, talk," I said once we'd settled with our stuff at a table.

But Marina's mouth was full. She ate like she hadn't tasted food in days.

"You okay?" I asked.

She nodded.

"Still living with your aunt?"

She nodded again, this time rolling her eyes to let me know she still thought her aunt was a dopey sap.

"Man," she finally said after she'd swallowed half the croissant. "This is good! Want some?"

"What I want is for you to talk to me. What's going on?"

"That's what I want to know. What happened?"

I frowned. "What do you mean?"

"Did the cops keep you all this time?"

"What do you know about me and the police?"

"Remember—you promised you wouldn't get mad."

"What am I supposed to not get mad about, Marina?"

"About last night. Or I guess it was this morning."

"How do you know about last night?"

She shrugged, hesitated, then offered me a tentative smile—a please-don't-hit-me kind of smile that tugged at my heart. "I—I saw the cops talking to you."

"You were there?" I felt my anger rise. "Why? What are you—you're following me now? Come on, Marina. I thought we were friends. What are you doing? Spying on me?"

She cast her eyes down and sat very still, like a little rabbit crouched under a rock hoping the wolf won't notice it. Her fingers held the croissant over her plate, but her hand didn't move.

"When you're friends with somebody, Marina, you go places *together*. You don't *tail* your friends."

She lifted her eyes and they were full of remorse. "I was worried about you."

"Right."

"No, really. I—I—Remember that time I was telling you about how every December I always get real depressed because that's when my parents died, and even though I was just a little baby, it always makes me think about them? And do you remember what you said? You said you always get sad like I do, except for you it's in April."

"So?"

"So I remembered that. And it's April and I was worried."

"I never said when in April."

"You said you always go to where the accident happened. You said I ought to do something like visit my parents' graves or the house where they died or something like that in December just to check in with them. You said it would make me feel better if I did something like that. And it did."

"So why were you tailing me last night?"

"I told you—I was worried. Aren't friends supposed to look out for each other?"

"Looking out is one thing, tailing's another."

"You promised you wouldn't get mad," she said.

"Okay. I'm not angry."

She watched me for a second, then said, "I went to the library like you showed me how to do that weekend it rained and I looked up your parents' accident. It said where it happened and it said it happened at two in the morning. It said you go there every year, so I just snuck out of the house last night and I waited."

She sat quietly, watching me for signs of forgiveness. But I'd quit listening. I was thinking of something else. I studied her tired, dirty face and tried not to smile.

"You saw it, didn't you? You saw them dump the body."

She hesitated, then nodded, and the excitement I'd seen when I drove up colored her eyes again. "Yes," she whispered. "Yes. I saw the whole thing."

5

"One of them reminded me of my uncle Jake," Marina said in the car on the way down to the Hall of Justice.

The last time I'd seen Jake Murieta, he'd been dead and under water for days.

"How so?" I asked, trying to push the awful vision of what was left of his mutilated, scummed-up, and bloated face out of my mind.

"He was little and wiry like Uncle Jake."

"Was he Latino?"

"Yeah. So was the other guy. Only he was fat and sweaty. He was wearing a Harley Davidson T-shirt and a windbreaker. And the guy like Uncle Jake was wearing a pea coat and red cowboy boots."

"That's great, Marina. The cops might really be able to find this guy because of you," I said.

Marina smiled back at me, but it was one of those sort of absentminded smiles, the kind you use when you're not really listening, when you're thinking about something else.

She fingered the bag I'd made her dump the rest of her pastries in, looked out the window for a minute without speaking, then said, "You know what? I bet the cops won't do anything."

"Why wouldn't they?"

"They don't care. All they ever do is drive around school and rag us for not being in class. They, like, stopped Joe and Paco the other day an' patted them down in front of everybody. It was dumb. All they care about is harassing kids."

She plopped the bag of pastries on the floor, crossed her thin arms, and slouched down in her seat with a dramatic pout. "I'm not talking to cops."

"Yes, you are. If you know something about a homicide and don't tell them, they can charge you with a bunch of stuff." I didn't tell her they had to find out you were withholding first.

"I won't be a snitch."

I pulled my eyes off the traffic and glanced across at her. "Do you know these guys? The ones who dumped the body?"

She squirmed. "Uh-uh."

I turned back to the traffic in time to avoid hitting a red Miata in the process of running a stop sign. "You can only be a snitch if it's some-body you know, Marina. What you're going to do is be a witness."

"But—"

"No *buts*, Marina." I pulled to the curb across from the Hall of Justice and jammed the gearshift into park. "Come on. Bring your muffins and let's go. You're going to do your civic duty."

6

hecker, or maybe it was Marks—I was still having trouble remembering who was who— listened patiently while Marina munched her cupcakes and reluctantly described the two guys who dumped the handsome but nerdy guy on the grass behind me. He jotted a couple of things down in a notepad he'd slapped onto the nicked-up interrogation-room table when he came in, but he looked like he was losing steam fast.

"What about the vehicle, young lady?"

"My name's Marina."

He made a face, then glanced at me. "Okay. Ma-*reee*-na. What about the vehicle, Ma-*reee*-na?"

She shot me a venomous look, then said, "It was a van. A dark blue van."

"Make? Model?"

She shook her head.

"Foreign? Domestic?"

"What's that supposed to mean?"

I could tell she thought he was getting at

saying something nasty about her Mexican heritage.

"Was it made in the U.S.—like a Chevy or a Ford Econo or a Dodge? Or was it a Mitsubishi, Volkswagen, like that?"

Marina looked exasperated. "I said I didn't notice, okay? So stop asking me."

"Okay." Checker—or Marks—hoisted himself out of his chair and opened the door. "Thanks for coming in, Marina. And thanks for bringing her, Ms. Ventana. If either of you remembers anything else, give me or Officer Checker a call."

Marina went through the door like a bullet, but I hung back. "Did you find out the guy's name?" I asked.

"Yeah. John Doe."

"His fingerprints didn't match up?"

"Nothin's matched up," he said wearily. "But maybe your young lady's tip'll get us something."

"Was it a blunt instrument?"

"Huh?"

"The murder weapon. You said the M.E. thought he died from a blow to the head."

He gave me a queer look. "I told you that?"

I nodded. When he didn't answer, I said, "Well?"

He sighed and ran a pudgy hand over his sagging face. "Let me put it this way: My life would get a lot simpler if a witness stepped forward and said he saw our Mr. John Doe back into a baseball bat last night."

I caught up with Marina at the elevator.

"That guy's a creep," she said.

"Yeah?"

"Yeah. And he's stupid! How's he ever going to find out who killed that man if he's so stupid?"

"What makes him so dumb?"

"He just *is*, that's all." She popped a stick of gum into her mouth and started chewing.

"Marina, if you're going to be a private investigator, you're going to have to learn to get along better with the police."

"Why? You don't."

"Sure I do."

She gave me a baleful stare and stepped into the elevator. "I think *we* should investigate."

I followed her in and punched "1" on the panel. Marina waited a few seconds in silence before she realized I was ignoring her question.

"Are you too busy?" she asked.

As the elevator hummed downward, I thought about my caseload. I had a deadly boring insurance case—something about worker's-comp fraud and a strained back. I was supposed to catch the goof lifting something, which meant I'd have to go sit in front of his house in Concord waiting for him to mow the lawn or something. Otherwise my calendar was open.

"Look, Marina, even if I was going to look into this thing, I wouldn't include you. You've got school."

"School's boring."

"Maybe it is. But you're going to need it if you want to work with me."

"How am I ever going to know if I really want

to be a private investigator unless I try it out? I think we should solve this case. Then I'll know."

"An open homicide? I don't think so."

We reached the Toyota. Marina was quiet until we pulled out and headed toward the Mission. "Where are we going?"

"I'm going home to get some sleep. Then I'm going out to Concord to work an insurance-fraud stakeout."

"Can I come?"

"*You're* going to school."

"Aw, shit."

"You need a note to cover this morning?"

She didn't answer, so I drove on in silence until we hit Mission High. When I stopped at the front entrance, Marina reached for the car door.

"Hey," I said.

She looked over at me, still sulking.

"You didn't leave anything out, did you, Marina? When you talked to Checkers?"

Her big black eyes blinked at me. "Like what?"

"Like a lead, Marina."

"That would be dumb," she said, then smiled, threw open the door, and scampered down the walk to the school entrance like a kid heading for an ice-cream stand.

7

I didn't think any more about the dead guy for the rest of the day except for the three calls on my answering machine from Marina trying to badger me into investigating his death. After a couple of hours of sleep I drove out to Concord and nailed the insurance cheat in record time with a big, fat shot of him lifting a twenty-five pound bag of charcoal briquets into his car outside the Costco. I got video and still shots—all in two and a half hours flat.

As I drove toward the City, I had a weird feeling somebody was following me. I tried a few tail-breaking maneuvers, like crossing eight lanes at the tollbooth, taking exits, then getting back on the freeway, and making U-turns once I hit city traffic, but none of it turned up anybody. Maybe I was just getting paranoid. Then again, maybe whoever was following me was really good.

I dropped off the video camera and tape at the insurance company, told them I'd get them the written report by tomorrow, and drove home. Standing on the sidewalk, about to let myself into my apartment building, I heard somebody call my name.

I glanced over my shoulder to see who it was, but nobody was looking at me. People were walking by—tourists, city dwellers, a couple of regulars from the neighborhood I knew well enough to nod good morning to—but nobody had that expectant look you see on people's faces when they're waiting for you to respond. I glanced down the street in both directions. Nothing.

Then out of nowhere a bulky, bustling man came rushing toward me.

"Ronnie! Ronnie Ventana. *¡Que sorpresa!* What a surprise!"

I blinked. The solid, gray-haired man took up the better part of the sidewalk in front of me. His suit had to have cost him at least a thousand dollars, and his face looked fresh and pampered, like somebody who's just had a facial. The effect was the same crisp, barbered but slightly jowly look of John Gotti. He backed away, smiling, nodding, holding his arms out to me.

"What's the matter?" he said, feigning offense. "You forgot your father's old friend, Diego?"

He grabbed my hand and started pumping it, then pulled me into a quick embrace. My nostrils filled with a rich, vaguely musty scent—pipe tobacco, which I'd always associated with my parents' attorney. And with the smell my head filled with memories. I felt fourteen all over again.

"It's been too long, *mi bonita*, hasn't it? 'Cisco would never forgive me."

"Sure he would, Diego. You know he was a softie when it came to you."

"Hah!"

I smiled and looked him over. Diego Torre was more polished, a little grayer, and a lot stouter than when I'd last seen him six years ago. But he still smiled the same. "How are you, Diego?"

"Ashamed. Ashamed and contrite for not having called or checked in on you before. And look how we meet—by accident! *¡Que verguenza!*"

"I'm not fourteen anymore, Diego. I—" But he wasn't listening. He'd turned to look up and down Grant Avenue. "Do you have a moment, *bonita*? Come, let's find a café. We will raise an espresso in memory of your lovely parents."

He took my elbow and steered me down the street, past the Quarter Moon and around the corner to Columbus. We ducked into Café Roma, where we ordered cappuccinos. Then he said, "Now, *preciosa*, tell me what you've been doing with yourself."

"Sure, but first, how's Magda and the kids?"

"Ah, you know Magda." He threw up his hands in mock exasperation. "*No cambia*. She will never change. I could get Charles Manson paroled easier than I could convince Magda it's time to retire. She works too hard, you know? Those delinquents at Mission High don't want to

listen to the old-lady civics teacher anymore—
they want to score, they want booze and girls and
boys and parties. You know what Magda says?
She tells me five of her kids last year got college
scholarships to study political science. Ivy
League!" His pride showed even as he shook his
gray head. "Imagine that!"

When our coffee came, he said, "Now, what
about you? Still working with those unfortunates?"

The parolees were "unfortunate" because
they hadn't been blessed with a lawyer who could
get them off—a lawyer like Diego.

"Not exactly." I pulled a business card out of
my pocket and slid it across the table. He held it
up to the light, then dropped his jaw dramati-
cally. He'd feigned the same kind of pleasant
surprise when I practiced magic tricks on him
as a kid.

"A private detective! *¡Ay, bonita! ¿Pero qué es
esto?*"

Looking at him, a wave of sadness washed
over me. He was aging so gracefully. The brash
young trial attorney was now a stately man, comfortable and pleased with life, pleased with himself. Would my parents have aged so nicely? I
wondered. Would they have been mellow, or
would their illicit lives have led them to ruin and
despair? Somehow I couldn't picture it, but I
couldn't help but wonder.

Diego tucked the card inside his breast
pocket and patted the spot where it lay, then
declared it was a *maravilla* that we had run into
each other because, with his heavy work load,

he might have let another year go by without seeing me.

"Speaking of which," I said, rising, "I've got to go. I've got a report to write."

"Of course, *bonita*. Of course."

After we said our good-byes, I trudged home, feeling sad and oddly bereft, missing my parents more after seeing Diego than I had last night before my vigil got sidetracked with the body. I slipped the key into the lock, went upstairs, and drank three beers while I started the report I was supposed to turn in with the video. I didn't finish the report, but somewhere around three in the morning I did manage to finally fall asleep.

!

was surprised the next morning when Checker phoned.

"We got your suspect," he said tersely. "Picked him up a couple of hours ago."

"Did he say who the dead man is?"

"My life should be that easy. We're trying to get the kid down here to I.D. him, but she says she won't come unless you bring her."

Marina was just playing hard to get. When I picked her up at Mission High, there was a small between-classes crowd of kids hanging around. And I got the distinct impression they were all hanging around because she'd told them who I was and where she was going.

They stared extra hard at me when she opened the car door, and as we drove off they stared after us like we were going to the promised land. At least they were half right about that—whatever we were headed for, it had to be more exciting than Algebra.

Marina's eyes danced with excitement. "We got him," she said.

"*They* got him. Maybe."

"No maybe. That cop Checker said he was in the blue van. And he was still wearing those stupid red boots. That '*mano* must be a real dope to keep wearing those boots like that. It's not like they stand out a mile away or anything. He's pretty dumb."

"Let's not convict him yet."

Marina frowned.

"You've got to make sure he's the same guy you saw," I said. "You don't want the wrong man to go up for this."

"But—they got him."

"They picked up a man driving a blue van. He was wearing red cowboy boots. That doesn't mean he's the one who killed that guy."

Marina frowned. "But you said—don't you want to solve this murder?"

"I just want you to be sure."

Marina nodded somberly and rode the rest of the way staring out the window in silence.

But when we got to the Hall of Justice, Checker and Marks were all smiles and apologies. They said they were sorry but we'd made the trip for nothing.

"What do you mean?" I demanded.

They stuck to the it's-all-been-a-big-mistake-and-the-guy-we-brought-in-is-the-wrong-guy story for a good five minutes. They didn't finally cave in until I said, "Marina's the only one who saw him. Right?"

Checker nodded wearily.

"So how can you know if he's the right guy or not?"

"He's got an alibi. It checks out. Trust me, he's not your guy." Marks looked annoyed that Checker was still even talking to me, much less explaining anything. I tuned him out and focused on Checker.

"Maybe the alibi's covering for him," I said. "Let Marina see him. You may get two criminals for the price of one."

Checker seemed to be actually considering it, but Marks just shook his head.

"Sorry, Ms. Ventana. Can't do that."

"What's it going to hurt?" I asked, motioning toward Marina, who'd plopped down sulking on a bench across the hall the minute she smelled resistance. "Marina's here. She's willing and ready. What if this is the guy?"

"What if it isn't?" Marks said.

I smiled. "Then you'll be sure."

After a heated, whispered huddle down the hall the detectives came back and said Marina could look at the guy, but it wasn't going to be a lineup or anything. The suspect was by himself in an interrogation room and we'd go into the side room and look at him through the one-way glass. They were doing it informally and this was just to get us out of their hair and I needed to be clear on that, that once we looked at the guy, that was the end of it and don't come back until and unless they called us in to I.D. somebody else. Then Marks said something about how he'd think long and hard before he ever called me again.

Marks hadn't even closed the viewing-room door before Marina cried, "That's him!"

She shrank back, eyes wide, covering her mouth with both hands. The scrawny man smoking at the scarred-up table had a gashlike dimple in his chin and angry, confident eyes that burned like two windows to hell. He looked capable of violence and he looked capable of enjoying it.

Marks put his hand on Marina's shoulder and pushed her roughly up toward the glass again. "Look again," he ordered. "Are you sure?"

Marina shook the guy's hand off her shoulder and composed herself. She'd shown fear, and fear is something that costs you dignity, especially in the barrio. I caught her eye.

"Are you sure?" I asked.

She stared back with an assurance I'd never seen before, then turned to the policeman. "Positive," she said.

Checker and Marks exchanged grim looks, but Marina didn't seem to notice.

"What's his name?" I asked as they scuttled us out into the hall like we'd just told them the guy was a vampire.

"We're not at liberty, Ms. Ventana," Marks said, and kept us moving away from the interrogation room.

"Where'd you pick him up?" I said.

"Thanks for coming in," Marks said brusquely, then started to turn away.

"Hey, wait."

Marks wasn't going to stop, but when Checker did, Marks stayed with him.

I looked at them both. Marks seemed angry, but Checker was definitely shaken.

"So what's the deal?" I asked. "Who is that guy?"

Neither one of them answered.

"What's the matter? Is he connected? Should we be looking out? What's the rest of the story here?"

"We'll be in touch," Marks said.

I turned to Checker. "It's better if I know."

Checker nodded, but he didn't say a word. Standing there, wagging his head up and down, he looked like a Humpty-Dumpty version of those spring-necked fake dogs people used to put in the back windows of their cars.

Marks said, "There's nothin' to know, Ms. Ventana. Like I said, we'll be in touch."

9

Checker and Marks vanished back inside the room next to Interrogation, and Marina and I started for the elevator.

"I told you they don't care," Marina muttered. "Cops never listen. That man probably paid them money to say he didn't do it."

Before I could come up with something positive to say, a chunky but well-groomed man thundered down the hall toward us. He was about fifty, with a small, stingy mouth and coal-black hair slicked down from a side part. He had that perverted, avaricious look some D.A.'s are born with. *That must be why he looks familiar*, I thought, but I couldn't place him. The guy scurrying alongside him was slender and wore glasses. He looked federal.

The chunky guy stormed toward us, then pulled up short and stared, eyes narrowed, boring into me. I slowed my pace and stared back while Marina shrank away against the wall to watch first him, then me.

"What's your name?" the chunk demanded.

I straightened my shoulders. "What's yours?"

"I'm City Prosecutor Harland P. Harper."

"Shit," I said. It just sort of slipped out. Over by the wall, Marina giggled.

Harper nodded, and the look on his face was like a doctor's zeroing in on a diagnosis of the plague. "Your name's Ventana, isn't it?"

I straightened my shoulders some more and raised my chin. "That's right."

Before I could say more, Checker and Marks popped out into the hall and blanched when they saw us talking with Harper. Marks rushed over while Checker vanished through the same door the slender federal guy had just gone through. Marks nodded at the city prosecutor. "Mr. Harper. We're down here."

He tried to direct the prosecutor down the hall, away from the interrogation room, but Harland Harper didn't budge. Full of indignation, he turned to Marks. "Do you know who this is?"

"Uh—" Marks looked at me like he wished I'd never been born.

"She's related to those cat burglars."

"Alleged," I said.

Harper squinted at me. He seemed to stop breathing. "What?"

"Alleged cat burglars, Mr. Harper. In case you forgot, my parents died before you could finish prosecuting them. And you know what they say, Mr. Harper: innocent until proven guilty. Does that ring a bell?"

His mouth formed a snarl. He looked like he was going to say more, but instead he waved a chunky, manicured hand in dismissal and nearly knocked Marks over as he charged down the hall after Checker and the federal guy. Marks scowled at me, then hurried after him.

"Wow," Marina said. "He really hates you."

"He doesn't even know me, Marina. What he hates is the fact that my parents died before he could build a career on prosecuting them."

Marina frowned. "He looks pretty big-time to me. Isn't he the one running for supervisor or something?"

"Mayor. But it's all relative. Maybe he thinks he could have made it to the White House if he'd gotten the chance to put my parents away."

I started down the hall, and Marina followed.

She said, "In civics they're like, he's way ahead of Martinez, and that's supposed to be bad news for the Mission. They're like, we should all get our relatives out to vote. And I'm all, yeah, right, like my stupid *tía* is going to make a difference?"

I punched the elevator button, and the doors sprang open. "Your civics teacher isn't giving you the whole story, Marina."

She slouched into the elevator behind me with a what-else-is-new expression on her dusky features.

"Harper isn't just bad news for the Mission," I said. "He's bad news all around."

10

"Welcome back," I said when Lieutenant Philly Post called me later that afternoon. I'd picked up the still shots of the doofus lifting bags at the Costco and was busy finishing up the report so I'd get paid.

Post grunted. Or maybe it was a growl.

I said, "I heard you were on vacation."

"Who told you that?"

"Checker. Marks."

"Uh, yeah. Well, listen, I—"

"So where'd you go?"

"When?"

"On vacation?"

"No place special. Look, Ventana, I'm calling about this John Doe thing."

"Are you taking over the case?" I'd had enough of Marks and Checker's squirrely behavior.

"Huh? Uh, no. Look, something's come up."

"What?"

"I need you to come down. We'll talk about it."

"Why don't you just tell me over the phone and I'll decide if we need to talk?"

"It's about the kid."

"What about the kid?"

"Come down and I'll tell you."

Thirty minutes later I was sitting across from Post. He looked pale and haggard, not like somebody who just got back from a holiday.

"Where'd you go on vacation?" I asked. "You don't look rested at all."

He didn't answer.

"So?" I said, crossing my legs and giving him my best full-cooperation smile. "You wanted to talk?"

Post's expression didn't give anything away. "This John Doe," he began.

"Right. Marina Murieta and the John Doe."

"Uh-uh, Ventana. *You* and the John Doe."

"Me? What are you talking about?"

"Tell me about him."

"He's dead," I answered.

Post's eyebrows quivered. "Cut the crap."

"You mean he's *not* dead?"

"You expect me to believe you're some innocent bystander in this thing?"

"I am."

"Bullshit."

"If this killer's telling you different, he's wrong. I never saw the guy before, Post. Never. The dead guy *or* the killer."

He was making me nervous. Last time I'd found a corpse, Philly Post had me locked up. If that's what he intended to do, he wasn't tipping his hand. He just stared, so I tried again.

"I don't know anything about this, Post. Honest." I raised my right hand. "I swear. Besides, why would I?"

He glowered at me. "You mean to say this guy gets dumped in your face and you don't think it's somebody sending you a message?"

"Is that what your guy's telling you? It's a message?"

"Answer the question, Ventana."

I'd already thought through and discounted the message angle. I wasn't working on anything but the dull old insurance thing. Worker's-comp fraud. Sure, some people got worked up over insurance, but I honestly couldn't picture the doofus at the Costco setting up a hit. If somebody was sending me a message, I would have had to recognize the dead guy. I would have figured it out. And I would have known what the message was and who it was from.

"What is this guy telling you?" I asked. "Message about what?"

"Hell if I know, Ventana." He drew in a deep breath and softened his voice. "I need you to play this one straight with me."

"I am."

Post blinked.

"I'm telling you the truth, Post."

"I find a link, Ventana, anything, any tiny little thread ties you to this stiff, you can kiss your license good-bye."

"If I'm lying, I'll *bring* you my license. On a gold platter."

"I'll hold you to that," he said gruffly, shuffling papers around on his desk. He found a folder, opened it, then looked up at me with the usual scowl. "Now, about this kid."

"Marina."

"Yeah. The I.D. was informal, not the way it should have been done, and my men know better. But it doesn't matter. She's not going to stand up."

"What do you mean? Marina's solid. She's not going to back down."

"Doesn't matter. Kid's school counselor says she does drugs, cuts class. Says she's unreliable."

"Unreliable?" That was lawyer talk for liar.

"She's been going around telling people she's Dario Murieta's daughter."

"So?"

"So Dario Murieta is the Mexican consul general. He's not pleased."

"Maybe they're related."

"Nope. We checked. She's been making up stories about an aunt who's a movie star. She even told one teacher her grandmother was Rita Hayworth and her real father is Howard Hughes. When the teacher pointed out Hughes has been dead too long, she said they used frozen sperm."

"Have you talked to her about it?"

"What's she gonna say that's gonna make a difference? The kid's a liar. Her uncle was a hit man. Who's gonna believe her? Bottom line—her word's not going to stand up in court. Between her reputation and her uncle's, our guy walks."

"Is this because Harland Harper is involved?"

Post's expression didn't give anything away. "Where'd you hear that?"

"I heard it, that's all."

Post stared at me for a beat, then threw his head back and laughed. It was a quick, sharp bark without any humor. "Nice try, Ventana."

"If he's not involved, what was he doing down there?"

"Where?"

"Outside."

"Outside where?"

"It—well . . . in the hall."

"You saw him in the *hall*? Come off it, Ventana. The man *works* here. You see him in the hall and suddenly it's a conspiracy? Jeeezus!" He made a face. "You got bigger problems around this guy than I thought."

"Are you saying he's not involved?"

"Not even close."

I stared hard at Post, trying to penetrate his inscrutable expression. He *could* be telling the truth. "What's the innocent guy's name?"

Post frowned. "Leave it alone, Ventana. I'm only telling you this to give you a heads-up. So you'd know the kid's feeding you a line."

"Maybe she is. But I'd still like to talk to the guy."

"Talkin' to him's not gonna make your kid a credible witness."

"Maybe she won't need to testify."

Post scowled. "What are you thinking,

Ventana? He's got an alibi, and the only person who can place him at the scene is a compulsive liar."

"The alibi," I said. "I forgot about the alibi. That pretty much kills it, doesn't it?"

Post hesitated, then said, "It's tight, Ventana. She's impartial and eighty-five years old. D.A. checked it out: He was home all night."

Something amid the mountainous mess on his desk made a loud buzz. He scratched around a pile of papers, plucked a phone out of it and said, "Yeah?"

While he listened, he squeezed the bridge of his nose with two fingers. Then he said, "I'll be right there."

When he replaced the receiver and looked up, he acted surprised to see me.

I said, "It's the landlady, right?" His mother or grandmother wouldn't be impartial. And who else could vouch for him all night?

Post rose wearily from his chair, reached for a jacket on the hanger behind the door, and said, "Look, Ventana. I just did you a courtesy here. Why don't you do the same for me."

"Since when is asking somebody to butt out a courtesy?"

He slid his arms into the jacket and adjusted it onto his broad shoulders. There was a tear at the corner of the breast pocket, and the cuffs were frayed.

"Fine," he said. "Go ahead. Believe the kid. Doesn't change my job. But know this—" He jabbed the air with his index finger. "I catch you so much as breathing around this case, I'll bust you for interference. Got that?"

"But—"

"Drop it. And I mean now."

11

I went downstairs fuming. When the elevator opened onto the lobby, I headed for the front door, then stopped. Marina was sure of her I.D. And I was sure of her. So how could this guy have a legitimate alibi? He couldn't. But Post wouldn't lie. Or would he?

I went over to the bank of pay phones, pulled out Officer Checker's card, and dialed.

"Checker," a voice answered.

I looked over my shoulder to make sure nobody was around to overhear, then said in my most official, clipped tone, "This is the D.A.'s office calling to see when you're available for a meeting to discuss some additional information we've acquired regarding the John Doe case suspect."

"Herbie Caballos?" He sounded puzzled—no, incredulous. I could just picture his bulging eyes clouding over with confusion.

I said, "Herbie who?"

"Caballos. Is that who you're talking about? 'Cause if it is, he's clear."

"Uh—oh, yeah, right. Maybe it's the landlady. What's her name?"

I heard papers rustling on the other end, then, "Mrs. Trujillo?"

"On Balboa Street, right?"

"Balboa? She's on Florida Street. Jeez!" Checker's voice rose. "What's going on over there? You guys lose the file or what?"

"This *is* the homicide at Ocean Beach we're talking about, isn't it?"

"Ocean Beach? Try Sunset and Santiago. Look, get it straightened out, and if you have to, call me back. Better yet, call Marks. He's workin' this damn thing too."

I hung up and had just started for the doors when I heard, "Ms. Ventana! Yo!"

I scanned the milling crowd of lawyers, civil servants, and their loser victims. A shriveled, jockey-sized guy in a cheap suit was scurrying toward me, waving and grinning at me like I'd just told him he'd won a million dollars. He didn't look familiar, but he seemed to know me, and from the level of his enthusiasm, my guess was he liked me. A lot.

As he came nearer, I saw his shirt was yellowed and stained down the front on either side of a narrow, ragged tie. And the dark suit was worn shiny in spots. If he paid more than twenty bucks for it—new—he was robbed. A tattoo of a red and black rooster covered the back of his outstretched hand.

"It's Cocky, Ms. Ventana. Cocky Burnett! You gotta remember me. You were my P.O."

Cocky Burnett. The last time I'd seen him, he hadn't had any teeth. His hair had been bowl-cut down to his jawline, and he'd just blown three months of parole by sticking up a liquor store in the Haight with a water pistol. Now he had a nice, even, but gray set of dentures and a crew cut.

"Cocky," I said without enthusiasm.

"Life's lookin' up, Ms. Ventana." He smoothed his lapels, then patted them smugly. "I'm doin' good."

Most cons don't enjoy making appearances at the Hall of Justice unless they've got a fix on the judge. Cocky might have been street-smart, but he'd never struck me as the influential type. I glanced pointedly at our surroundings.

"Oh," he said, shaking his head earnestly and smiling. "I know what you're thinkin', Ms. Ventana, but it ain't nothin' like that. I'm here to *testify*. I'm testifyin' for the *prosecution*."

He stepped in closer and lowered his voice. "They pay good," he confided. "It's steady."

"How can one trial be steady?"

"One trial? Oh, no." He chortled like I'd just told him the funniest joke he'd ever heard. "I'm connected good. Anytime I'm runnin' low, need ta pick up some change, I drop a dime." He grinned and puffed out his chest.

"You're ratting people out?"

His smile faltered. "It's good, honest work, Ms. Ventana. You parole officers are always pushin' good, honest work."

"Snitching on people isn't 'good, honest work,' Cocky. Nobody respects a stoolie."

"I'm not a stool," he said petulantly. "I'm a *government witness*. I'm puttin' bad guys away. Thought you'd be proud."

"It sounds like a scam, Cocky." Just like everything else he'd ever done.

"Then how come the D.A.'s giving me money?"

I considered asking him if he'd done any snitching for Harland Harper, then thought better of it. Cocky Burnett was the kind of guy who'd take my enquiry upstairs and sell it.

"I'm doin' a bona fide good deed here, Ms. Ventana. Every time I testify."

"Somehow I don't think the defendants look at it that way. Have you been doing this long?" Word on snitches usually travels fast.

"Been a while."

"Why do the defendants keep talking to you?"

He puffed up and some of the old bravado returned as he chuckled. "Let me put it like this: I got ways," he said, then glanced at his watch. "Gotta go. The good guys are expectin' me."

12

Herbie Caballos and his landlady lived in a tiny house on Florida near Twenty-second Street not far from Marina Murieta's house. Somebody had planted roses out front and glued a statue of some saint to the wood above the doorbell. Even though every other house on the block was trashed, theirs was meticulously painted and well kept. And the yard was clean. The place didn't look like a murderer's house.

When Mrs. Trujillo opened the door, I saw exactly what Post had meant. He said she was Caballos's perfect alibi. And she was. Tiny and fragile-looking with a head of fluffy white hair pinned back in a bun, she had the benevolent smile of an angel.

"*Buenos dias,*" she said warmly, and I was sure she'd opened the door without even checking to see who'd rung the bell.

"Mr. Trujillo?"

"*Sí, soy yo,*" she said. "I am *Señora* Trujillo."

"My name's Ronnie Ventana. Could I talk to you for a minute? It's about Herbie."

"Herbie's not home," she said. She was still smiling—a good sign.

"I'd like to talk to you, if you don't mind."

"*Sí, sí. ¡Como no!* Would you like to come inside?"

I followed her down a short hall into a doll-sized living room. There was a divan, a chair, and an enormous television set tuned to a game show. The sound was off, but the words on the gameboard were in Spanish. She motioned for me to sit on the divan, then picked up the remote and switched off the television.

"*Ahora,*" she said. "You want to speak to me about *mi inquilino*—my tenant?"

"I understand he was home with you last Tuesday night?"

She nodded. "He is a good boy. He is quiet and he pays the rent every month. I know if something bad happened it would not be the fault of Herbie. He is so polite. He takes me to the *mercado* whenever I ask. He is a good boy."

"Does he live here in this house with you?" The place didn't seem big enough for one person, much less two with secrets between them.

She nodded again. "He has a room downstairs. He sleeps there. And Tuesday night, at two in the morning, he was in his room."

"Are you sure about that? Weren't you asleep?"

She smiled patiently. "Sleep does not come as easily as it did when I was young."

"Did you see Herbie? Was *he* asleep?"

"Come," she said, rising slowly from her chair and beckoning me to follow her. "I will show you."

We walked toward the back of the house, to the kitchen, where she stopped at the sink and looked out the window.

"I was reading," she explained. "In my bedroom. The history of Ecuador. And my bedroom, it is directly above Herbie's room. I could hear his music playing. At ten o'clock and again at two o'clock I came into the kitchen to take my *medicina*." She patted her bosom where her heart lay. "*Mi corazón*, you see. That's how I can be sure of the hour. I stood here both times as I do every night. If Herbie is home and his light is on, a little square of light appears on the neighbor's wall. Right there."

I followed her gaze out the window to the neighbor's wall next door. "You saw his *light*?"

She nodded. "When his light is on, I can see the reflection there."

"But you didn't see him?"

"The light was on. He was there."

"And that's what you told the police?"

"I didn't speak to the police, *señorita*. I spoke to the *abogado*."

"From the D.A.'s office?"

"Yes."

"What was his name?"

She frowned and closed her eyes for a minute. When she opened them, she shook her head and then said, "I am sorry. I cannot remember."

"Could you describe him?"

"Oh, no. We did not meet, *señorita*. The *abogado*, he telephoned. We spoke on the *teléfono*."

Great. Another thorough investigation by the D.A.'s office. "Do you mind if I take a look outside?"

"*Sí*. Of course. Please."

She unlatched three crummy little locks I wouldn't have used to secure a doghouse and led me out the back door. On the way to the side of the house, we passed a small entry leading underneath the house.

"Is that Herbie's door?" I asked.

She nodded and smiled, so I decided to press my luck.

"Mind if I take a look inside?"

"Oh, no, *señorita*. We could not do that. Herbie does not like others inside his room unless they are invited."

If I were a murderer, I'd have the same policy. I turned my attention back to the yard. It was small and well maintained, like the front, and there were a couple of Adirondack chairs in a sunny spot in the corner. Around the side of the house was Herbie's window, low and close to the ground and covered with wire mesh.

Down the walk toward the front of the house was a gate leading to the street. Herbie had free come-and-go access to his little private room downstairs. I'd seen all I needed to see.

13

"The landlady can alibi Herbie Caballos's bedroom light," I told Post. "She can't alibi him."

Philly Post dropped the sheaf of papers in his hand, and his perpetual scowl deepened. "Where'd you hear that name?"

"Never mind where. Listen to what I'm saying. Herbie Caballos's alibi is no good."

"What are you talking about, Ventana?"

"Don't play dumb with me, Post. Herbie Caballos. You said the landlady was his alibi."

"So?"

"So I went out and talked to her, which is more than anybody in this department did. She says Caballos was home because his light was on. She didn't see him, though. And she didn't hear him. He wasn't home, Post. His alibi doesn't stand up."

Post blinked. "Didn't I tell you to butt out?"

"Yes. And I'd like to know why."

Post's expression was unreadable except for the coldness in his eyes. "I don't have to tell you squat, Ventana."

"I know you don't *have* to. I thought maybe you'd *want* to."

Post drew himself up and eyed me carefully. "You tryin' to say something here?"

"I see two possibilities: One, maybe the D.A.'s office has got some sloppy investigators." I paused. "Or maybe somebody around here's taking care of this guy."

He stared.

"All I'm saying, Post, is there's something screwy about this deal. Can't we talk about it?"

"Do I look like Internal Affairs?"

"You look like Homicide, Post. Or at least you used to. Don't you want to solve this case?"

He didn't answer.

"Is Harland Harper holding you back?"

"Harper? Jeezus! Harper's got nothing to do with this."

"Will you swear to that?"

"Your kid made a mistake, Ventana. Face it. Face it and stop trying to make something out of nothing. Let me do my job."

"And what job is that, Post? Did they scratch 'solving homicides' off your job description while you were gone?"

This time his face flushed a deep purple. He shot out of his chair and, through gritted teeth, said, "I got more stake in clearing this thing than you do, Ventana. This is my *job*. Now, I told you to butt out and I mean it. I catch you within a mile of any of these people, I'm locking you up for obstruction. Now, get out. Get out of my office now before I throw you out."

14

The phone was ringing when I walked into my apartment. I grabbed it before the machine picked up, but whoever it was hung up. The indicator light was blinking, but before I could press Rewind and listen to the message, there was a knock at my door.

I crossed the room and peeked through the peephole. Blackie Coogan, my best friend, mentor, and fellow P.I., stood out in the hall, lighting a cigarette and sort of growling under his breath. I thew open the door.

"Ready?" he said, blowing smoke into my apartment from where he stood.

I checked out his clothes for a clue as to where we were going, but he was wearing the usual—worn leather jacket over jeans and a worn, button-down shirt. "For what?"

"Dinner. A.A.P.I., remember?" He pronounced it "ay-pie." The American Association of Private Investigators.

"Come on, doll. Let's book."

Fifteen minutes later we pulled into the parking lot at Gabbiano's. Blackie shut the engine off, but he didn't get out. He reached for a cigarette, lit it, and squinted at me while smoke billowed over our heads.

"Fucker eighty-sixed you, huh?"

He was talking about Post. I'd just finished telling him about my latest encounter.

"I coulda told you, doll," he said.

"Well . . ."

I rolled down my window and stared at a sailboat dipping its lights out in the blackness of the Bay. Fog filtered gently into the car, pushing out the smoke and wrapping itself around my face like a damp, welcome kiss. Across the seat from me Blackie kept his sexy blue eyes turned on me. There was just the mildest curiosity in his expression. He knew there was more.

"It feels like a cover-up," I finally said.

Blackie grunted noncommittally. "Sounds like he's bein' the same asshole he's always been."

"Maybe. But things don't add up here. Why take this little old lady's flimsy alibi? Why doubt Marina's rock-solid I.D.? I don't get it. It doesn't click."

"Fuckin' cops, doll. You know the game. Maybe this guy Caballos is workin' an angle. Maybe he gave somebody up. Maybe he's got somethin' on one of the cops."

"Harper," I said, almost to myself.

"Post's the asshole givin' you the vibe."

I looked up. "But Harper showed up when Marina I.D.'ed Caballos."

Blackie drew deeply from his cigarette, then blew the smoke out in a curlicue ring over our heads. He glanced at me and squinted, then casually asked, "Harper the guy tried to put the Burglars away?"

"This doesn't have anything to do with him trying to prosecute my parents, Blackie."

He flicked his cigarette out the window.

"Had to ask," he said, then splayed out the fingers of his raised right hand and closed them in a fist, watching his hand as it moved. I'd never noticed before how big his knuckles were.

"Whatever," he said, dropping his hand into his lap. "Who gives a fuck?"

"Besides, that's not my motive," I insisted. Sure, I hated Harland Harper's guts, and in some strange, convoluted way I sort of even blamed him for my parents' death. They were both skilled drivers but as the trial neared, they'd begun to drink more and more. The night of the accident, I was sure they'd been drunk. But that didn't color my instincts on this. At least I didn't think it did.

Blackie glanced toward the restaurant. Through the open window I could hear the waves slapping against the pilings below the pier. A seagull screeched somewhere nearby.

"You set on this dinner?" Blackie asked.

I laughed. The speaker was probably done by now, and the old farts in the audience were most likely winding up to retell their old war stories again for the hundredth time.

Blackie reached for the ignition and cranked the engine.

"Fuck 'em," he said. "Fuck Philly Post. Let's bust some chops on this."

15

When we hit the Mission, we headed for
Florida Street, then parked just far enough
down the block from Herbie Caballos's
house so that we could see it as we sat in the car.
Salsa music filtered out from somebody's lighted,
open garage behind us and warmed the darkness
around us.

Blackie eased himself back against the seat
and reached for a smoke and a match. We'd
decided on the way over that we'd start conserva-
tive—with just a stakeout. Sometimes you can
learn a lot about somebody just by watching
where he lives, where he goes.

I sipped the last dregs of a cup of stale coffee
we'd picked up on the way and tried to ignore the
rumblings in my stomach. Somehow the now-
cold pizza slices we'd bought and stashed atop
the pile of junk in the backseat had lost their
appeal. What I really wanted, given the neighborhood, was a couple of enchiladas.

"Fat boys get a clue on the stiff yet?" Blackie asked after we'd sat for a while.

I'd talked to Checkers about the John Doe after Post had thrown me out. "Nothing. It's strange, isn't it? You'd think a guy like that would have a girlfriend or a boyfriend or a wife or somebody who'd report him missing."

"No I.D.?"

"According to the cops, they cleaned him out. But here's the thing—why haul him around in a van and dump him? Most of those guys usually just leave their victim bleeding on the street where they nailed him, right? They don't drive them around the city."

"That's the usual dance."

"So this wasn't a stickup. But why? Why haul him around like that? Why dump him?"

Blackie started to answer, then went tense. "Heads up, doll."

I followed his gaze and saw a figure come toward us on the sidewalk. The guy was big, broad in the shoulders, and he moved like a lumberjack. He was the antithesis of the wiry guy Marina had I.D.'ed in the interrogation room.

"That's not him," I said.

Blackie relaxed. "Suppose he shows?"

"I don't know. If he's alone, we talk to him. Find out what he's like, let him know he might have the cops covered, but we're on to him."

"And if he's got company?"

"We keep watching."

Blackie made himself comfortable, then reached into the backseat. "Want a slice?"

•   •   •

Private-detective rule number thirty-seven says if you've got to set up a stakeout, let the cops know about it. That way you won't get rousted when the neighborhood snoops and biddies call in to report a suspicious person hanging around. The problem is usually I'm working something the police would prefer I wouldn't work anyway, so it's counterproductive to tell them what I'm doing. And tonight was no different.

But a couple of hours later, when a dozen Latinos with biceps the size of hams showed up out of nowhere and surrounded our car, I regretted not phoning in. The biggest one demanded our I.D.'s.

"Nothin' doin'," Blackie said.

They were all wearing red-, white-, and green-striped bandannas on their sleeves—the colors of the Mexican flag.

I rolled my window down and smiled at the bruiser on my side. "I'll show you mine if you show me yours," I said.

If they'd wanted to rob us, they would have already. The guy nodded and reached into his back pocket while I scanned the swarthy faces surrounding the car. It was nighttime, but I could make out the features of a few of them. None of them was Herbie Caballos.

The guy flipped a pseudo official-looking laminated card in my face. I didn't read his name; what jumped out at me was Las Casas Neighborhood Watch Angels. My smile got broader.

"Neighborhood Watch," I said. "You guys keep an eye on things?"

"The I.D., *señorita. Por favor.* We will have to call the police if you do not tell us who you are and what you are doing here."

Beside me Blackie twitched. He was ready to start the car and mow down the guys blocking our path. I caught his eye, shook my head imperceptibly, then slipped my P.I. license out of my pocket and handed it to the lug at my window.

"*¿Y del hombre?*" he said, nodding toward Blackie.

I knew Blackie. He'd die like a dog in the street before he'd give them so much as a match. "Forget him. He's my driver."

The guy looked at the card in his hand, then at me, then back at the card.

"Ventana?" he said. There was excitement in his voice. Then somebody came up next to him and shone a flashlight in my face. Somebody else spoke. The voice sounded distant, but it was only because I couldn't see anything behind the glare of the light.

"Ventana," the voice said, like it was confirmation, and a whole buzz went up around us.

"*Mira a la cara.*"

"*Tiene que ser la hija,*" somebody else said.

An older guy, maybe in his fifties, bent down past the light to look through the window at me.

"*Se parece,*" he said, then grinned.

Beside me, Blackie cursed. "Lose the fuckin' light," he said.

And they did. Blackie was angry, but nobody

seemed to notice. They were all staring at me.
The guy outside my window beamed, then said,
"Forgive me, *señorita*. We did not know. But you
are the daughter of 'Cisco Ventana. *¿Verdad?*"

When I nodded, they all cheered and started
to rock the car. "What the *fuck*?" Blackie
demanded.

A couple of guys shouted something that
ended with the word *cerveza*.

"Beer," I said, translating one of the few
Spanish words I know. "I think they want to buy
us a beer."

16

When I woke up, it was daylight and I was at home, curled up on my unopened sofa bed with a headache the size of the Pacific. I couldn't remember how I got home or what, exactly, I'd done.

There was some vague memory about tequila and something about celebrating the memory of my father. *Chihuahua*. That was it.

Most of the neighborhood-watch guys were from the Mexican state of Chihuahua—where my father was born. The older one had even known him. My dad beat him at pool one night during the trial. The guy had made it a big point to tell me about how my dad had sworn to him on his mother's life that he was innocent of the charges against him. "Others," my father had told the guy, "other thefts perhaps, but this—this is *una locura*. It is pure fabrication. I had nothing to do with this."

My father had said the same thing to me.

The rest of the evening—Blackie leaving near the end with a showy, big-busted woman named Conchita, the bar closing down, the swirling spiral of a ride home in somebody else's car— started to come back to me when the phone rang and split my head wide open. I lunged before it could ring again, managed to knock the receiver off the hook, then picked it up off the floor and sort of moaned something I hoped would sound like hello.

"*Señorita* Ventana?"

"Uh."

"This is Lucho Navarro. I hope I am not disturbing you."

"It's not a real good time," I muttered, cradling my still-pounding forehead carefully in my palm.

"I will be *breve*, then, *señorita*. I only wish to reiterate my offer of last night."

"Your offer?" I tried to think for a minute, but the effort made me nauseous. "Who are you?"

He started to explain, but I cut him off.

"I remember now. You bought the first round last night."

He was the older guy in the group, the one who'd known my father, the one who'd told me he was innocent. "Tell me again, you said my dad talked to you about the trial?"

"*Sí, ¿Como no?* It was an evening I will never forget. The great 'Cisco Ventana playing pool with Lucho Navarro. These things, they do not happen often."

"About the trial," I prompted him.

"Yes. He swore to me that he did not commit this crime of which he was accused. He said he would not be convicted because he did not take the necklace. Those were his exact words. I will remember them until I die. It was only a coincidence that I was there at the Gallo Prieto that evening. Just as it was last night that I should meet you, *Señorita* Ventana. And I believe there is a reason for this."

His voice had a rhythm that soothed my pounding brain. It kept me listening.

"I understand you cannot discuss *la investigación*, but it is obvious that there is a connection to my neighborhood. Please, I wish you to reconsider the offer to you that I made last night."

"Which was?"

"If I may be of assistance to you in *la investigación*."

That's all I needed. A bunch of amateurs running around messing things up. I'd already asked him about Caballos. I remembered now. Nobody in the group knew anything about Caballos, but they knew his landlady. She'd started renting out the room downstairs sometime last year, after her husband had died.

"Thanks, Mr. uh—"

"Navarro. Lucho Navarro. *¡A la orden!*"

"Mr. Navarro, I appreciate your offer, but I think Blackie and I have things under control right now. I'll call you if things change."

I started to hang up.

"El Gallo Prieto," he said.

"What?"

"Where we were last night. You can leave word for me there anytime. I will be proud to assist."

17

Once I took about five aspirin and chugged a couple of triple-strength coffees, I felt better. Eating was out of the question, though, and so was calling Blackie. But investigating wasn't.

I spent the rest of the day doing the rounds in the Mission District, asking some of my ex-parolees—none of whom were amateurs—about Herbie Caballos.

Nobody had ever heard of the guy, so from there I went to the neighbors. The handful I questioned didn't know much. A couple told me he'd moved in six months ago and was rarely around. Somebody else ventured that he could have been dealing drugs, but when I asked her to elaborate, she just shrugged and said, "Doesn't everybody?"

By seven o'clock I was starting to believe that maybe the cops were right. Maybe Herbie Caballos was clean. And if I was thinking that, I clearly needed a break.

I stepped into a cantina off Valencia, ordered

a Dos Equis, and found the pay phone. There was only one message on my answering machine—from Marina's aunt.

"This is *Señora* Murieta, Miss Ventana," she said in heavily accented English. "I am so sorry to trouble you, but do you think it would be possible for you to come to my house?"

Marina's aunt was a limp-rag kind of person—the type who'd managed to drift through life without ever making a move or a decision of her own. Marina's tirades against her spinelessness had, rightly or wrongly, colored my opinion of her, so I was feeling sort of reluctant to get sucked into some petty family drama.

But I set my beer on top of the phone, fished out a couple of dimes from my pocket, and dialed. While the phone rang, I let the warmth of the beer wash through my system. My limbs felt heavy as they started to relax.

"*¿Bueno?*"

"Mrs. Murieta? This is Ronnie Ventana."

"Ah, *Señorita Ventana. Gracias a Dios que llamó.* It is Marina." She stopped abruptly, and I heard a snuffling, hiccuping sound that ended in what sounded like a sob.

"What is it?" I said, not sure whether to be annoyed or alarmed.

"She has been in her room all day. She will not come out. She will not eat and she will not speak to me."

"Is she sick?"

"No, no. It is not that. It is something else, but I do not know what."

I got there five minutes later, and Mrs. Murieta burst into an encore of tears and histrionics. I ignored her theatrics and asked for Marina, so she dried up and led me to a closed door in the back part of the house. She stood there beside me, a dark, bandy-legged woman smelling of onions and garlic, snuffling into a lace handkerchief while I knocked.

After a couple of seconds without a response from inside the room, Mrs. Murieta pulled me aside.

"You must go in," she whispered. "Marina will not speak. She will not say, 'Come in.'"

She made little urgent motions with her hands, indicating the bedroom door. *"Andale,"* she said, and started sniffling again. "Please. *Por el Dios santo.*"

I knocked a second time. "Marina? It's Ronnie, Marina. Can I come in?"

"Ronnie?" The voice didn't sound at all like Marina's. It was small and frightened, but Marina's aunt's dark-skinned face lit up.

"Go," she urged. "Go inside and speak to her."

"Can I come in, Marina?"

There was a long pause. "Okay. Just you."

I left the aunt standing at the door and stepped inside a darkened room that was stuffy and dank, the size of a closet. The barest bit of light from a streetlamp outside seeped through the cracks on either side of the drawn shades. I had to blink to adjust my eyes. Then I looked around.

There was a dresser and a nightstand and a twin bed all crammed in so close you had to walk sideways to pass between them. Clothes were strewn on every surface, and amid the shadows I could make out a couple of rock-band posters hanging on either side of the small window. Marina was crouched against the wall on a narrow twin bed in the darkest corner.

"Hey," I said softly. "You okay?"

She shook her head.

I took a couple of steps but had to stop because my knees bumped the end of the bed. "What's going on?"

She shook her head again, but this time she made a small snuffling sound.

"Hey, tell me about it, Marina." I sat down gently on the edge of the unmade bed. From there, in the dim light, I could see that she was clutching a pillow against her small, flat chest and that her eyes were big circles of exhaustion.

"Swear you won't tell anybody," she whispered.

"What's this about?"

"I can't say it unless you swear first. He said not to tell anybody."

"Who? Did somebody threaten you?"

She shook her head again, and suddenly her face crumpled. She let out a big sob.

"It was Caballos, wasn't it?"

She shook her head violently. "I'm not supposed to say."

"What did he do to you? Marina, tell me."

"H-h-he held a knife to my throat," she sobbed. "He said he would k-k-kill me."

"Was it Caballos? The guy you I.D.'ed?"

"Y-y-yes."

"He's not going to kill anybody," I said angrily. "What did he want? What did he say to you?"

"H-he told me if I ever went to the cops again, I was d-d-dead."

"Where? When? When did he talk to you?"

"Out front," she began haltingly. "Fernando gave me a ride home. He dropped me at the corner like he always does so he won't have to go around the block 'cause his car doesn't have reverse. I was walking up the steps to the porch an' he jumped out. I didn't even see him. I don't know where he was. He scared me so much I couldn't scream or nothin'." She punched the pillow clutched to her chest, angry. "An' besides, what's my stupid old *tía* gonna do anyway if I screamed? He had the knife. I tried to kick him, but he backed me up against the wall and stuck the knife under my chin. And that's when he said what he said."

She took a deep, quivering breath and put a hand against the front of her neck, like she was remembering. I studied her mottled face in the dark, trying to stay cool through my own anger.

"We've got to go to the police," I said. I was willing to swallow my pride. If Post wouldn't listen, I'd go over his head and talk to his captain. If they didn't care about Marina or the dead guy, somebody somewhere in the big bureaucratic tangle that was the S.F.P.D. had to care about solving the case. But Marina wasn't buying it.

"Why should I?" she demanded.

"We can put this guy away for assault."

"They won't believe me. It's like he said. Nobody believed me the first time. They'll just think I'm making it up. And then he'll kill me."

"Are you going to stay in your room for the rest of your life?"

She cast her eyes down.

"Look, if you don't want to go, I'll talk to the police myself."

"No!"

"It'll be unofficial, okay? I'll take it to Post."

"He's the one who called me a liar."

"I'll talk to him, Marina. I'll get him to understand."

Her tired eyes flashed. "I wish my uncle was alive. He'd take care of this *pendejo*."

"Only if you paid him, Marina. Your uncle did that kind of stuff for money, remember?"

She stared at the darkness beyond the window while her fingers clenched and unclenched the pillow held to her chest. After a moment she said, "You swore you wouldn't tell anybody."

I didn't answer.

"You *swore*, Ronnie."

"What if I told you, what if I *promised* you, that if Post doesn't do anything, I'll take care of Caballos myself?"

Her eyes sparked. "How?" she asked eagerly. "Are you going to kill him?"

"I don't kill people, Marina. I'm a P.I., not a hit man."

I wanted to say something more, to convince her the police were the ones to take care of it, but they were the reason she was in trouble now. Bedsides, it was too late. The despair deadening her eyes when I first walked in was back. Fear and rage contorted her face into something ugly.

"Go away!" she cried, burying her face against the wall. "Leave me alone. You can't protect me. Nobody can."

18

I had to wait until eight o'clock the next morning to do it, but I tried the legal way first.

Post wouldn't buy it. "The kid's a pathological liar," he said, unmoved.

"You've never even talked to her."

"Checker and Marks did. They're top-of-the-line cops."

I thought about the big hole in Herbie Caballos's alibi. "Right. I guess you're basing your opinion on the great job they did making sure Caballos's landlady had laid eyes on him when she swore out his alibi, right?"

His dark eyes snapped with anger. "Look, the kid's just making this up, Ventana. If you want to chase your tail on it, go ahead, but I'm not going to bite. My advice? Lose the kid, she's nothing but a headache. Maybe there's something there between the two of them, but we'll never know the truth. All I can tell you is, Caballos is clean."

"Because Harland Harper says so?"

Post scowled. "Because he's clean, Ventana."

"If he is, it's probably because he's threatened witnesses to everything he's ever done, just like he did Marina."

Post sighed. "If that's the way you want to see it, go ahead. You're not changing my mind."

"Fine," I said, gathering up my backpack and heading for the door.

"Ventana!"

I paused, hand on the doorknob, and turned to face Post's junked-up office. He sat at his desk, holding a case file in one hand, a stern expression on his usually unreadable face.

"Don't get any ideas."

"Too late, Post. I've already got the idea you don't want to help."

"Leave it alone. I'm lookin' at it from the outside, Ventana. That kid's got you snowed."

19

"So what's the plan?" Blackie asked.

It was two o'clock in the afternoon and we were driving out to the Mission District. Blackie was happy. Knowing I was angry enough to defy Post made Blackie so happy he was whistling.

"All we're going to do is go in there and talk to the guy. You're my goon-power, okay, so look nasty and evil. And if his landlady shows up, flirt with her."

We were close, about three and a half blocks away from his house, when we drove past a blue van with its window rolled down. I noticed it because I thought it might be Caballos's, but I didn't see anybody inside and I couldn't be sure, so I didn't say anything.

At the tidy little house on Florida Street, Blackie and I went to the side gate and rang the bell. Nobody answered, so I rang again and waited. Nothing.

Blackie drew deeply on his cigarette, then glanced across the yard to the front door of the house.

"Let's try the back," I said.

As I stepped through the low gate, I patted the small leather case of lock picks in my pocket. "Who knows? If he's not there, maybe the latch on his door didn't exactly catch when he left."

Midway to the backyard, down along the side of the house, Blackie froze. I heard a quick rapping sound from somewhere over our heads. I looked up, and Mrs. Trujillo's worried face appeared in the window above us. Then she recognized me and lifted the glass.

"Herbie is not home," she announced in a kindly voice. She looked frail.

"When do you expect him?"

"I don't know. He did not come home last night."

Either that or he didn't turn on his lights, I thought. "It's kind of important, Mrs. Trujillo. We need to talk to him."

"*¿Qué pasó?* Is something wrong?"

I glanced around at the neighbor's house next door. There was a movement in the window. "Can we come inside?"

Her gaze followed mine and she understood immediately. Nodding, she said, "*Sí, sí, como no. Pase por atrás, por el pátio.*"

"She wants us to go in the back way," I told Blackie.

Blackie grunted and headed down the path. Mrs. Trujillo held the door open for us to go inside, then, after I'd introduced Blackie, she led us into her tidy little living room and we all sat down.

She wore a brightly colored dress today and rubber-soled shoes, the kind waitresses and nurses use. Her white hair was gathered in a braided bun at the base of her neck. She looked solemnly at Blackie, then at me.

"There is something wrong?" she asked, and for a fleeting moment I considered telling her about Herbie's threats to Marina. If I thought she had any influence with the guy, I would have.

Instead I said, "It's important that we talk to Herbie. Does he have any friends? Somebody who might know where he is? He might be with one of them."

"Herbie is a good boy," she said with conviction.

Blackie and I made noises of agreement.

"Herbie did not kill that man," she said.

"We don't want to talk to him about the murder, Mrs. Trujillo. It's something else."

"What?"

"Out of respect to Herbie, I think he'd prefer that we talk to him about it first."

She studied me for a moment, then Blackie. "I think there is something bad between you and Herbie," she said to me. "You do not believe he is a good boy."

"I don't even know him," I said.

"*No importa.*" She drew herself up and raised her chin. "I am sorry, *señorita, señor,* but I cannot help you. I do not know where Herbie is.

And it is not as if he were a little boy in school and I know the names of his friends."

"Would you at least tell us where he works?"

She rose and stared down at us with cold dignity. "I do not know. Perhaps you will leave me your telephone number. I will ask him to telephone you when he returns, yes?"

20

Out in the car Blackie cursed. "Old bat knows the fucker's got something to hide. She's scared, did you see that?"

"She seemed more defensive than scared, Blackie. Nobody wants to be told they've rented the spare room to a killer. She's going to hold on to that 'Herbie's a good boy' line until she sees him bludgeon somebody to death herself. And maybe not even then."

Blackie started the car.

"Drive back the same way we came, will you?" I said. "Past that empty lot."

"Yeah?"

"Right, turn up." I pointed. "Over there."

The dark blue van was still parked in front of the overgrown vacant lot. A brick factory building across the street was boarded up. The rest of the buildings looked abandoned too. There were no pedestrians, not even any bums hanging around. The spot was as secluded as you can get in a city.

The van's window was still wide open. The block was beyond the self-appointed jurisdiction of the neighborhood-watch group—otherwise I was sure they would have noticed the vehicle and probably called it in to the police.

"Pull over by the van over there."

"Think it's Herbie's?"

I shrugged. "It's worth checking out."

When Blackie stopped, I jumped out of the car, walked up to the open window, and peered inside. There was an alley cat sitting on what looked like a pile of old clothes lumped together across the front seat. I leaned in for a closer look and something grayish-white caught my eye. It looked weird and out of place.

I leaned in farther and squinted to see what it was, then gasped. It was a hand. A human hand hung out of a sleeve and rested on the center console next to an empty Styrofoam coffee cup. The fingers curled slightly as if its owner was asleep, only the skin was a weird blue-gray. It didn't look real.

And there, right beside the cat's bobbing head, where he was lapping up something dark, I could make out an ear. A human ear attached to a—a—I wheeled around and ran a few steps toward the back of the van, then bent over and heaved.

Blackie was at my side in a minute. "You all right, doll?"

"Fine," I said, then wiped my mouth with my

sleeve and tried to quell my lurching stomach by taking in a deep breath and looking at the sky. It was a soft blue-gray, pale, just like the dead guy's hand.

"Oh, God," I said. And then another wave of nausea hit me.

When I joined the living again, I heard Blackie behind me yelling at the cat. "Scat!" he said, then cursed. "Shoo, you little fucker!"

I looked up. Blackie's head was stuck inside the van, hands clutched behind his back so he wouldn't leave any fingerprints. I considered joining him, then lost my nerve and walked over to the far side of his car and leaned against it, waiting, sucking in deep gulps of air and trying to erase from my mind every vivid detail of what I'd just seen.

When he came up beside me a few seconds later, Blackie's face had a greenish cast.

"Fuckin' cat," he said, and cursed some more. "Clean shot to the head. You see a gun in there?"

I shook my head.

"Me neither. Think it's Caballos?"

"I don't know. Did you see red boots? Red cowboy boots?"

Blackie grimaced, then started toward the van. "Anything else?"

"Pea coat. A blue pea coat."

There was a long silence behind me, then Blackie was beside me again. "We got him," he said. "Let's blow."

While Blackie scrambled behind the wheel, I stared at the pavement and wondered why

Herbie Caballos would take his own life. Then I thought a moment and wondered *if* Caballos would take his own life. I hadn't seen a gun, and neither had Blackie.

"Ventana! Wake up, come on! Let's *blow*!"

Back inside the car I watched Blackie twist the key to the ignition. I felt dull-headed, heavy.

"He's definitely dead," I said.

"As a doornail, doll." Blackie rammed the car into gear and stomped on the gas. The car shot down the block like a rocket.

"He won't be hasslin' your kid anymore, that's for sure." Blackie's face was grim. "Think he felt remorse? Or you think he just felt the bullet?"

"Did *you* see a gun?" I repeated the question he had asked me.

"Huh-uh," Blackie said.

I thought for a minute. "He could have fallen on it, you know, afterward."

We turned left, then right, and continued straight. With every inch of distance we put between us and the van, my head seemed to get clearer. It took me a couple of blocks before it sank in that we'd have to depend once again on San Francisco's finest for a judgment on whether Caballos had taken his own life or had it taken from him. The same cops who still hadn't been able to identify the man from Sunset Boulevard, who'd been deaf to Marina's testimony and blind to the weakness in Caballos's alibi. Somehow I couldn't muster much faith that they'd call this one right either.

"Turn back," I said.

Blackie stared at me for so long he almost rear-ended a green Pontiac in front of us. "What?"

"Turn back. I want to take a look inside that van."

21

"You sure you got the stomach for this, doll?"

I stepped gingerly around the mess I'd made on the pavement earlier.

"I've got nothing left to lose," I said, patting my roiling but empty stomach, then pulling on a pair of oversized work gloves Blackie had dug out of the pile of trash on the floor of his car. Blackie stayed with the car and kept watch.

On the drive back I'd decided to look in the rest of the van, too, while I was there. And now that the moment was upon me, I decided to do that first.

The back door of the van was locked, so I took a second to jimmy it open. A gust of fetid air hit me and almost sent me to the curb again, but I gave it a couple of seconds to air out, then breathed through my mouth and stuck my head inside. From where I stood at the back bumper, I could glimpse part of the prone hulk that was

Herbie Caballos between the two bucket seats.
Would I have the nerve to actually touch him—
it? I averted my eyes and focused on the rear part
of the van.

There were a couple of faded, flower-
patterned bedsheets tossed in one corner, three
bunches of bundled old newspapers scattered
around on an oil-stained brown carpet, a suitcase, and three grimy cardboard boxes.

I climbed inside for a closer look. The suitcase was empty except for a tiny bar of hotel
soap. The first box had some tools in it, a few
empty cans of beer, crumpled fast-food wrap-
pers, some aerosol carburetor cleaner, and three
quarts of oil. The second one had about a hundred pristinely preserved *Playboys* wrapped in a
plastic bag. And the third, the third one looked
like a gold mine—old bills, canceled checks, and
an unused parking citation booklet.

I backed out of the van, dragging the third
box with me. It was heavy, but I made it to the
car and shoved it into the trunk while Blackie
kept watch from behind the wheel.

"Pay dirt?" he mumbled as I passed by him
on my way back to the van.

"We'll see."

I shut the van's back door. Blackie was still
keeping watch, but I glanced up and down the
street anyway just to make sure nobody was
coming. Down the street, cars drove past the
intersection, but none turned down Vermont
Street. The site was perfect for a suicide. Or a
murder.

I took a deep breath and headed for the front passenger side of the van. The door was unlocked. Too bad. I would have liked to put off getting up close to what was inside for just a couple of minutes more. But I inhaled again, then forced myself to open the door.

The alley cat was back. I focused on its angry face and tried not to look at anything else. It looked up at me and hissed.

"Scat!" I said, and waved my arms. It didn't move. I stepped back and looked on the ground around me. The sidewalk was clean. There was nothing I could jab it with. Great.

I took off my jacket and waved it frantically up and down like I was fanning a fire. When I opened my eyes, the cat was gone. I looked around. It was crouched in the back of the van on top of the piled-up sheets. The minute we made eye contact, it opened its mouth and let go an awful-sounding moan that made the hairs on the back of my neck stand on end.

I told it to shut up, and amazingly it did. Leaning gingerly into the interior, I avoided looking at what used to be Herbie Caballos while I reached for the glove box and opened it. No registration. No insurance record. Just a couple of receipts for car repairs. Two long hunting knives. An unopened pint of cheap whiskey. And a gun— a Saturday night special.

I rummaged around some more, but that seemed to be it. Then, as I started to shut the glove compartment, a tiny white something fell out and fluttered to the floor. I snatched at it and almost managed to grab it, but it landed in the gummy-looking pool of blood and serum on the floor mat below.

I stared. It was a torn scrap of paper with numbers on it. A phone number? Bank account? Gritting my teeth, I plucked it out of the muck and wiped it off on the back of the seat above Caballos's head. Then I took a good look at it. Seven digits with a dash after the third one. It *was* a phone number. Definitely a phone number. But the last digit was sort of smeared. I was in the middle of trying to make it out when a voice behind me said, "Whatcha got?"

I jumped, then spun around, heart in my throat.

"Blackie! What are you doing out here? You're the wheel. You're the lookout."

"Came to see what the holdup was, doll. Time to book."

He was right. We'd been there too long. I wiped the scrap of paper off one more time with my gloved hand, then stuffed it into my pocket. I shut the glove box, then turned to Blackie.

"I haven't moved him yet," I said, half hoping he'd offer to do it for me.

Blackie glanced past my shoulder at the interior of the van and shrugged. "Need to get the lead out," he said, then went back to the car.

I turned around and stared at the mound of ooze that had been Herbie Caballos's head. My mouth was dry and my head felt like it was suddenly someplace else, someplace cold and dark. *You can do it,* I told myself.

I held my breath and looked at the clotted mess. How much damage was due to the cat and how much to the bullet? I couldn't tell and I didn't want to know. I reached over and tried to lift him. He was heavy and stiff. Great. If I wanted to move him, I'd have to step into the van to get the right leverage.

I glanced over at Blackie. He was busy looking down the street. I stepped into the van, reached around for the guy's shoulder and yanked. His body slid enough for me to look underneath. Nothing.

So much for suicide. I jumped down, shut the door, and ran back to the car, dropping the gloves into the trunk on my way.

As Blackie rammed the car into gear, he said, "Yeah?"

"No gun."

"How 'bout that slip of paper you got? Anything there?"

"Maybe. We won't know till we find a phone."

22

We crisscrossed the Mission District, cutting through parking lots and doubling back until we were sure nobody was following us. When Blackie finally stopped, we were outside a run-down jazz club off Third over in China Basin.

Like a lot of nightclubs, it didn't have any windows. The graffiti artists had taken full advantage of the unbroken space and covered every inch of the wall with violent black and red and blue hieroglyphics. The pay phone on the corner looked like somebody had tried to burn it down.

"Hooper's," I said, reading the weathered green and red neon sign above the nightclub's door. "It's been a while."

"Not long enough," Blackie said. "But the phone's handy."

From the outside Hooper's looked desolate, but then it always had. Blackie had introduced me to the place years ago when Benny Hopkins and Treacher Bones used to jam there every night. The marquee announced a trio that was a lot of notches down from mediocre.

"Whatever happened to this place?" I asked.

"Stiles never got it together after the cops busted Treacher for shootin' up in the back room," he said. "Fuckin' yuppie-suits tried it for a while, drove out the good people so they could call it theirs. Got a kick thinkin' they were livin' on the wild side. After they killed it, they moved on."

That was happening to a lot of venerable hangouts around the city. I reached into my pocket and pulled out the little scrap of paper that had fallen out of the glove box. "This last number here, Blackie. Does this look like an eight or a six?"

Blackie glanced down at my hand while he fumbled inside his jacket for a smoke. "Try a three."

So I did. It turned out to be a beauty shop on Parnassus. I tried it with an eight. That number was disconnected. With a six I got a beeper, so at the prompt I punched in the pay-phone number, hung up, and called out to Blackie, who was standing at the curb studying a racing form he'd plucked off the dash of his car.

He looked up. "You get a hit, doll?"

"Maybe. It's a beeper. If anybody calls, they'll expect to hear a man."

I stepped away from the phone kiosk so Blackie could reach the phone if it rang. "Say you want to meet at—" I glanced over at the club to make sure they were open. "Feel like a beer?"

Blackie grinned. "Am I breathin'?"

"Okay—say to meet you here in—"

The phone rang.

"Say half an hour." That way he—or she—wouldn't have much time to think.

Blackie lifted the receiver and snarled, "Hooper's. Third Street. Thirty minutes."

Then he slammed the receiver down and turned to me, one roguish eyebrow raised. "Sucker shows, I'm buyin'."

23

Blackie and I took a couple of bottles of Anchor Steam out to the car, then drove around the block so we could park down and across the street from Hooper's. Then we sat, nursed our beers, watched the door, and waited.

People came and went, mostly rugged-looking blue-collar types, the same type of customer that had been scattered at tables and at the bar when we'd been inside. Everybody who went inside looked like he fit in. So we just sat in the car slouched kind of low, waiting.

After forty-five minutes Blackie grunted and shifted in his seat. "We got a no-show, doll."

"Let's give it fifteen more minutes."

He nodded imperceptibly to let me know he was okay with that. "And then what?"

I shrugged. "I don't know."

I didn't really want to report the homicide. As soon as the police found out about Caballos, a lot of doors would be closed. Blackie agreed.

"Bad move," he said. "Dopes'll just fuck things up. We can work it."

I didn't argue. "Maybe there's somebody down at the phone company who can help us track the beeper. Know anybody there who'd like a beef-up on their home security?"

Blackie chuckled, then set his empty on the littered floor of the car and reached inside his breast pocket for a smoke. "I'm gonna ask you something, doll. I don't know if you thought about it or not."

He struck the match, touched it to the tobacco, and breathed in the smoke. After he'd exhaled out the open window, he turned to me. He didn't smile. "I just want to know your take."

"Spit it out, Blackie. You're making me nervous."

"It's about our friend, the stiff back there. Any chance in your mind that neighborhood-watch group could have had something to do with it?"

I didn't understand him at first, then it hit me. "The Mexicans?" He was right—I *hadn't* thought about it. But I didn't have to. "Of course not. That's crazy. Those guys all want to be cops. Good-intentioned citizens—not a hit squad."

"They seemed pretty loyal to your family name last night," he said.

I met Blackie's gaze and said, "They wouldn't."

Blackie shrugged. "Had to ask, doll."

After a while Blackie said, "What blows me is

you asked around and nobody's heard of this fuck. *Somebody* oughta know somethin'."

"It could come back to me. I've got a couple of my exes"—I meant ex-parolees—"working it."

Blackie nodded.

"My guess is he was killed by somebody he knew. He was sitting in his van, probably last night, and he was supposed to rendezvous with somebody. Maybe it was a drug deal, who knows? Maybe he was getting paid for the John Doe job, maybe the bullet was the last installment. Whoever it was showed up—either on foot or in a car—and blew a hole in his head. His window was rolled down, so he was probably talking to whoever shot him, not expecting it. Otherwise why would he leave his gun in the glove box?"

"Van wasn't tossed."

"Right, so he wasn't robbed. The gun would have been the first thing to go. No, he was killed because—because—"

Before I could finish, a green BMW glided past us, then slowed and pulled to the curb in front of Hooper's.

"Here's our guy," I said, but Blackie had already seen him.

When the door sprang open and the driver got out, I craned my neck to see. His back was to me. A big white truck drove between us, and in the fraction of time that it took to pass, the man had turned full face in our direction. I took one look at him and gasped.

"It's him, Blackie."

The man scanned the sidewalk on either side of him. I stared at the slicked-down hair, the expensive suit, and the arrogant face.

"You know this guy?" Blackie asked.

"Not only do I know him, Blackie. I hate him. He's Harland Harper."

24

Harper disappeared into the club, and my mind raced. There could have been a dozen legitimate reasons why Herbie Caballos had Harland Harper's beeper number in his glove box, but I couldn't think of one. All I could think was, *They knew each other. They're connected.*

Blackie shifted beside me. "What's he get out of it?"

"Harper was there after Marina I.D.'ed Caballos," I said, thinking out loud.

"You sayin' the stiff back there was this guy's arm?"

"I don't know, Blackie. Maybe Harper got him off so—"

"—so he could waste him?" Blackie scowled.

"Why not? What if he hired Caballos to kill the John Doe, then murdered his own hit man?"

"The guy's not city prosecutor for bein' stupid, doll. He's not gonna personally spring the guy and croak him the next day. He was gonna do him, he'd low-profile the whole project, know what I'm sayin'?"

"Okay, so maybe Caballos is—was—just his snitch. They're still connected."

I pulled my eyes off the bar's front door and glanced over my shoulder at the mountain of junk piled across the backseat of Blackie's old Buick. "Think your camera's in there somewhere?"

Blackie reached under the seat and pulled out an old 35-millimeter camera with a telephoto lens. He checked it for film, removed the lens cap, and focused on the front door.

"I got a clear shot when he comes out," he said. "You want profile or front face?"

"Just nail him any way you can."

When Harper popped out the front door five minutes later, Blackie's camera snapped and whirred a couple of times.

"Got him," he said, then stuck the lens cap back on, shoved the camera back under the seat, and reached for another cigarette.

Instead of heading back to his car, Harper walked over to the phone kiosk and checked its number. He stepped back, then looked up the street in the opposite direction from where we sat.

"He's going to make us, Blackie," I said, slouching down even lower so that I was practically sitting on the thick mat of trash on the car floor. I peeked over the edge of the door panel and watched Harper wade into the sea of cars in the parking lot next to the bar. He pulled out a notebook and a pen and started at the back, walking from car to car, jotting down something for each one.

"What the fuck?" Blackie asked.

"He's taking down license numbers."

Harper moved methodically from the back to the front of the parking lot. Then, when he'd finished there, he started on the cars parked on that side of the street.

I ducked back down and turned to Blackie. "He thinks whoever phoned him is inside. He's going to go back and run the tags and see if anybody familiar turns up."

"Time to book," Blackie said, tossing his cigarette out the window and reaching for the ignition. I slouched down lower in the seat and we sort of snuck away while Harper was down the street, scribbling down the license number of a big dump truck parked by a fire hydrant.

25

We ended up dropping off the film with the two shots of Harper at one of those one-hour film developers off Union Square. Then we grabbed some beer and a pizza to eat in the car while we waited, and pawed through the stuff from the cardboard box I'd taken out of Herbie Caballos's van.

Maybe somebody'd been stupid, maybe we'd get lucky and find a motive or an explanation of what was going on between Harland Harper, Caballos, and the unidentified dead guy.

But the first thing I noticed about the bills and canceled checks I pulled out was that they didn't belong to Herbie Caballos. The name on everything was Arnaldo Contreras. And the address was out in the Avenues, not on Florida Street.

I passed one of the checks to Blackie and kept rummaging through the rest of the stuff, which proved useless: a toaster, a hand drill, and two cartons of menthol low-tar cigarettes.

"Ever heard of this guy?" I asked, stuffing the junk back into the box.

"Only Contreras I know's a bantamweight outta Costa Rica. Took Mighty-Lighty Johnson for the title in a second-round knockout last year. He's thirty-six one, last I heard."

"What's his first name?"

"Choo-choo."

"As in train?"

Blackie nodded.

"Great."

We tried the phone number on the checks first and got the phone company disconnect recording. So we then drove out to Thirty-second Avenue and asked around, but nobody out there had heard of Contreras. That's when I noticed that the dates on the checks all fell within a period of eight months, and the eight months had ended six months ago. And then I noticed one of the checks was made out to Lindsor Properties.

"I'll bet you five beers they're the rental agents for that house back there," I said as we drove down Geary.

Blackie grinned appreciatively and pulled to the curb when I spotted a pay phone.

"Sit tight," I said, then ran out to look up their address.

26

Lindsor Properties keeps an office in the Flood Building on Market—the same place Dashiell Hammett worked out of when he was a Pinkerton. We made it there just past five o'clock in the evening.

Blackie followed me to the fourth floor and lingered in the hall while I strode into the reception area. It was deserted, but the light was on in the inner office, so I went over to the door and knocked, then pushed it open.

The room looked empty. At least the big, upholstered chair behind the mahogany desk was empty. I stepped inside, then picked up on something rustling behind me. As I turned, I heard somebody in quick succession moan, then say, "Shit!"

There were two of them—a man and a woman, both red-faced and half-clothed—sprawled on a leather couch against the wall behind the door. The woman was on top, and the man was sort of bucking and lurching, trying to get her off him while he reached unsuccessfully for his pants.

"Get *off* me," the man sputtered.

But the woman was too busy trying to pull herself together to pay attention. She sat up, sort of straddling the guy, and pulled her blouse closed with one hand, then yanked at the tiny skirt hiked up around her hips with the other. The odds were against her, but she was trying her best to hold on to her dignity—and her balance. She looked me straight in the eye and said, "Who are you?"

The man bucked one last time and she fell against the back of the couch. He started to wiggle into his trousers as she flailed her arms and cursed.

"The door," I said, averting my eyes long enough for the guy to zip himself up and for the woman to right herself and pull down her leather miniskirt. He rose while she sat on the couch and struggled with the buttons of her blouse.

"I thought you locked the door," the man snarled at the woman. He smoothed his shirt with his left hand and I noticed the flash of a gold band against the light. The woman's fingers were bare.

"That's right," she snapped. "I'm supposed to take care of everything."

She leaned down and slipped her feet into a pair of black high heels and stood beside her lover. "We're closed," she said.

"I don't think so."

Her eyes narrowed. "Excuse me? Who do you think—Who *are* you?"

"My name's Ronnie Ventana. I'm a private detective."

The man seemed to deflate. "Oh, shit. That's just wonderful." He pushed his thinning hair off his forehead and looked disgusted. "I suppose Lurlene sent you."

"Actually, no."

I looked at him and wondered what the woman saw in him. Not only was he two-timing his wife, he was balding and skinny and moved like a lizard. And the baffled expression that settled on his face made him look like a moron.

"Your wife didn't send me, Mr.—" I glanced at the brass nameplate on the big desk. "Mr. Latch."

"Well, thank God for that." He let out a dramatic sigh and continued to straighten his clothes. Once he finished, he looked me up and down, lingering a beat or two at chest level, then smiled like he thought he was Clark Gable. "So why *are* you here?"

"Who cares?" the woman said, sensing competition. "We're closed."

I spoke to the man. "I need some information about a tenant of yours."

"Forget it," the woman said. "I told you, we're closed. Now, are you going to leave, or do we call Security?"

The man said, "*Trina*. Let's hear what she has to say."

"Why?"

He looked exasperated. "Do I have to spell it out?"

Trina's beautiful dark brow puckered below her bleached-blond hair. She thought for a minute, then through pouting lips said, "Yeah."

"Forget it," Latch said. "I'll explain later. Just shut up and let me handle this."

"Hey! You can't talk to me like that." Trina tossed her head and came close to stamping her foot.

"Just shut up."

Trina huffed out of the office, and Latch turned to me with an amused expression. Over the sound of slamming drawers in the anteroom, he said, "She'll get over it. Now, what were we talking about?"

He moved in close so that he was almost touching me.

"Infidelity," I said, holding my ground and staring back into his small dark eyes. A movement in the doorway caught my attention. Blackie filled the opening, taking in the whole scene with a sardonic look on his weathered face. Trina stood behind Blackie, sort of fluffing and patting her hair.

"This guy giving you trouble, doll?"

One look at Blackie and Latch's leering Lothario smile vanished.

I said, "We're fine here, aren't we, Mr. Latch?"

He kept his eyes on Blackie and nodded imperceptibly. "Yeah. Sure."

"I don't know how it happens," I continued,

"but the wife—it's usually the wife, you know—always finds out."

Latch backed up and licked his lizard lips. There was nothing suggestive in the way he did it.

"This was just an accident," he said, glancing at me, then at Blackie. He came as close as you can come to whining without actually whining. "I-i-it just happened. And Trina—well, I felt sorry for—"

"Let's get down to business, Mr. Latch, before I lose my lunch and my temper and put in that call to Lurlene."

He took another step back. "Uh-okay. Uh—of course." A tiny drop of sweat popped out on his temple.

"Arnaldo Contreras," I said.

He gave me an agonized look, like I'd asked him a trick question and Blackie was going to chop off his finger—or worse—if he didn't give me the right answer. "Do I know him?" he asked.

"*You're* supposed to tell me. He rented a place from you out in the Avenues six months ago. An Asian woman lives there now. He paid seven hundred a month."

That obviously didn't connect because a couple more beads of sweat popped up on his forehead. He looked like I'd just pulled the pin off a hand grenade and was asking him to catch it.

I sighed. "I bet he filled out an application," I said. "What do you think?"

Latch's eyes darted from Blackie to a row of file cabinets against the wall.

"Well?" I said.

He scuttled over and pulled open the top drawer, then ran a narrow finger along the tabs. In one fluid motion he yanked out a blue folder and offered it to me, then held on when I tried to take it.

"You won't tell Lurlene, will you?" The whine was back in his voice.

Blackie shifted his weight. Latch flinched and let go, then stood there, sort of cowering by the cabinet. "Please don't tell her. Take it with you," he added hastily. "It's a blue folder—that means the file's closed. You won't tell Lurlene, will you?"

From the doorway Trina snickered. "Big man," she said.

"As much as I'd like to clue your wife in, Mr. Latch, it's a free world."

I opened the file. Stapled inside the front cover was a handwritten receipt. Arnaldo had picked up his rent deposit in person. And in cash.

I looked up into Latch's sweating face. "What do you remember about this Contreras guy?"

"*Nada.* Nothing. Zip."

"You seem pretty sure of that."

"All I can tell you is he paid his rent on time."

"So you *do* remember him?"

He licked his lips, and his eyes darted to Blackie, then to the girlfriend. "How about it, Trina? Help me out here, will you? You remember this guy?"

"Fuck you, Harry," she said, and started out the door. I signaled Blackie to follow her, and the instant he left, Latch seemed to relax.

I said, "How can you know he paid his rent on time and not remember him?"

"I'd remember if he didn't. Deadbeats and troublemakers I remember. The rest"—he waved his hand in dismissal—"the rest I could care less."

I thought of John Doe. "Was he about thirty, thirty-five? Sandy-haired? Did he look sort of bookish?"

"I told you—I can't really remember the guy."

"Was he fat?"

"I told you—"

"Don't say anything. Just think for a minute." I shoved the open folder under his nose and said, "Look at this. Think back. Think about your impression of him. Did he—"

Latch stared at the scrawled, written application and suddenly let out an exclamation. "Hey! You know what he looked like? He looked like a thug. Black hair. Nasty—all business."

"Any distinguishing traits?"

"No—uh—wait. Yeah. He had a dimple in his chin, you know, like John Travolta."

"Skinny?"

"Yeah."

I stared at the blue file in my hand and felt my heart go heavy. Arnaldo Contreras was Herbie Caballos. And I had a sinking feeling the name Caballos was just as phony as Contreras.

27

The next morning, after I called a sulking, unresponsive Marina and told her in oblique terms that she wouldn't have to worry about Caballos anymore, I headed for the Hall of Justice. My plan was pretty simple. I had thought about Harland Harper during my morning run and about the fact that Caballos/Contreras had Harper's pager number and that Harper had shown up when Caballos/Contreras was arrested. If these two things weren't related, it was a pretty far stretch in the coincidence department. And even if Philly Post wasn't convinced, I was.

And since Caballos/Contreras was tied to the unidentified dead man via Marina's I.D., odds were pretty good that Harper was tied up with the dead man too. I could understand if he'd kill his own hit man. But why kill the John Doe in the first place? If I could find out who the dead guy was, maybe I could figure out why he died.

When I stepped into Homicide, Checker and

Marks were both sitting at their desks, telephones glued to their ears. Philly Post was mercifully nowhere in sight. The two detectives were so busy talking and listening and jotting things down they didn't even see me come in.

As I wove through the maze of desks toward them, I thought about how little either of these guys looked like a police detective. Checker could have passed for a supermarket bag boy or a gas station attendant. And Marks, well, Marks was definitely a step up—maybe he was the guy who delivered the bread. But even so, there was still that unmistakable something about both of them that spelled cop.

"And you know that for a fact, ma'am?" Checker asked while Marks just kept grunting into his phone and saying, "Uh-huh, uh-huh."

Finally Checker drew a big *X* through the last four lines he'd scribbled on his notepad and threw his pencil down on top of it.

"All right, Mrs. Lee," he said, then hung up and rubbed his fleshy face with both hands. "Thanks for nothing," he muttered.

I cleared my throat.

"Ah." He leaned back in his chair and laced his stubby fingers together across his wide belly. He looked harried and worn out, but he managed a small smile. "Got some good news for us, Ms. Ventana? We can sure use some."

"Does this mean you still haven't I.D.'ed the dead man?"

Marks lifted his bloodshot eyes for a

moment, then went back to listening and jotting and nodding into the phone.

Checker said, "We're going to run a description in the paper soon as we pull a breather here. Been tied up. Haven't caught the time. Me and Marks got our plates full right now—besides the Doe we got a dead kid down at the Wharf and three dead illegals in Golden Gate Park. And we're teaming up with a couple of other detectives on two drive-bys down in Visitación Valley."

But no dead man in a blue van.

I thought of the corpse rotting away in the sunny Mission District and wondered how long it'd be before they finally found him. Then I tried to picture what kind of shape he'd be in by then. Best not to think about it.

Checker exhaled and stroked his belly like it was some kind of pet. "Four happy days in the city. I never seen anything like it. The place is falling apart. No wonder I eat too many doughnuts."

"About the case—"

"Like I said, we still don't know who he is."

"I've been thinking." And I had—inspiration had struck.

Checker blinked. "Yeah?"

"It's about the way he looked. You know how sometimes you can tell what somebody does for a living just by the way he looks?"

"Yeah?" He hadn't moved, but I could tell he was interested. Maybe even excited.

"Well, don't you think this guy looked bookish, sort of professorial. What if he's a college professor or something?"

Checker puckered his lips and thought for a moment. "Kinda young for that, dontcha think?"

"How old does the M.E. say he is?"

"Early thirties." He paused. I guess he was running the math—four years of high school, four in college, and three more for a Ph.D. He smiled. "I guess that's old enough."

"Have you got a picture you could show around at the colleges?"

He laughed. "What? In my spare time?"

"Let me," I blurted. "I can do it. If it turns out to be a waste of time, it'll be my time wasted, not yours."

"Yeah?" Checkers glanced over at Marks. "You hear that?"

Marks said, "Hold on, Mr. Lucas," then covered the mouthpiece and stared at his partner. "What?"

When Checkers told him about my offer, Marks's eyes flitted in the direction of Philly Post's office. "Not a great idea," he said.

Checker sighed, then turned to me. "Will you excuse us for a minute?"

Marks spoke into the phone. "I got to put you on hold, Mr. Lucas. I'll be right back."

I stepped out of earshot while Checker sidled up to Marks's desk. He bent down to argue in a low, urgent tone until finally Marks waved his hand in dismissal and went back to the guy waiting on the phone. Checkers motioned me over.

"Give me an hour," he said. "I'll see what I can get off the M.E. But I'm going to be honest with you, Ms. Ventana. Once a homicide cools like this, things get pretty tough to crack. The first twenty-four hours—that's our window. After that, things get cold real fast."

I was supposed to leave him to his work then, but I stood with my back to Marks and waited.

Checker looked up from his notebook. "Yeah?"

"The guy with the van," I said, making a point of not using Caballos's name. Or the past tense.

Checker glanced quickly at Marks, then back at me. "He's cleared," he said. "Didn't they tell you that?"

"His alibi—"

"Can't discuss it. Open homicide."

"He's got some pull," I said.

"Who told you that?"

"Well, he's not in jail, is he?"

"I told you—he's cleared."

"Who cleared him?"

Something clicked behind his eyes, telling me I'd pushed too far. I smiled and shrugged and gave him the aw-shucks-I-was-just-asking routine.

He didn't smile back. "Look, Ms. Ventana, I told you I can't discuss the case with you or anybody else, so just drop it. You want a picture from the coroner, I'll get it for you. But lay off this other guy."

I left Checker working the phones and for a crazy minute considered hunting down Post and telling him about the dead Herbie Caballos. Then I remembered the time before last, when I'd found a dead body—a dead senator, to be specific—and Post had me locked up. Besides, I was still mad at him over not believing Marina.

I headed for the elevators and outside and ran into Blackie just as he was coming out of a bail-bond storefront a few doors down.

"Hey, doll," he said. "Been checking the wire on this Harper fuck. You doin' the same?"

I told him about the John Doe angle, then noticed a lean, short man in a cheap suit just past the bail-bond door. He stood with his back propped against the brick wall, waiting for something or somebody. It took me a minute to recognize the new Cocky Burnett.

"Excuse me a sec, Blackie." I started toward him. "Cocky!" I waved to get his attention.

He looked over quickly, panic in his eyes, then when he saw it was me, he relaxed. Every small-time petty chiseler is programmed to run whenever he hears his name, and Cocky Burnett had been primed to spring.

"Miz Ventana," he said, and collected himself enough to strut over and pretend like he hadn't been scared. Since the last time I'd seen him, he'd started to grow what looked like a goatee.

"Got a minute?" I asked.

Cocky started to smile, then noticed Blackie. He cut his eyes quickly to me, like I'd just betrayed him or something. Then he backed away a step or two. "You wouldn't be tryin' to set ole Cocky up for a shakedown, wouldja Miz Ventana?"

"Not even close," I said, then turned to

Blackie and waved. "Catch up with you in a minute."

Blackie waved magnanimously, so I stifled my revulsion, took Cocky Burnett's arm in mine, and started down the sidewalk. "Let's have a chat, Cocky. How about it?"

"Uh, uh, I don't know." He cast a nervous glance over his shoulder. "Who is that guy?"

"He's a friend I just happened to run into."

"So who is he?"

"He's nobody, Cocky. Forget about him. What we're going to talk about, now, *that's* important."

He glanced over his shoulder again, but Blackie had already disappeared inside his rusted old Buick. "Uh, sure, Ms. Ventana. I guess."

He sounded anything but convincing. After a couple of yards I said, "So how's business?"

He whipped his head around to face me, puzzled, suspicious, just a little surprised. "Huh?"

"Trolling for work?"

"I don't need to do no trollin'. Most times they bring it to me."

"They must think a lot of you," I said.

His tiny chest puffed out. "I'm reliable."

"That's what I figured. Listen, I need some information, Cocky."

"That's my business." The word *business* was my cue to cough up some cash, so I slipped a ten into his jacket breast pocket. The fabric felt coarse against my fingers.

Cocky patted his pocket and waited.

"Ever do anything with Harper?" I asked.

"Prosecuting attorney? Hah!" He stared at me with renewed interest. "You must be into something big. That's gonna be worth a bundle, huh?"

I shrugged, and a huge, greedy smile broke out across his sallow face. "You got somethin' for Harper, huh?"

"I don't have anything, Cocky. I just want to know if you've worked with him before."

"A man's connections, Ms. Ventana, is all he's got. I can't give away my confidential connections."

"Have you worked with him or not, Cocky?"

Cocky slowed down, serious now, all business. "You got something that big, what's my cut?"

"There is no cut. I don't have anything, Cocky. I just need to know if Harper uses sn— informants."

He sighed. "I gotta think on this one."

"There's nothing to think about, Cocky— either you have or you haven't. Look, I've got other people I can approach, but I thought since I know you, I'd talk to you first."

He pressed his mouth into a straight line.

"Well, maybe I overestimated you," I said.

"It's not that, Ms. Ventana. It's just you're talkin' about my livelihood here. I gotta protect my interests." He swung his clipped head around to glance quickly at me, then looked away. "Okay," he finally said. "Say, maybe I haven't. But that don't mean I couldn't set somethin' up with the guy. It's no big deal."

"Ever hear of somebody called Herbie Caballos?"

His sharp little eyes bored into mine. "Cop?"

I shook my head. "He sometimes goes by Arnaldo Contreras."

"Maybe. But yer better off with me, Miz Ventana. Me and you go way back. I wouldn't cut you wrong you bring something to me. You know that. An' who knows about the reliability of this other guy."

I reached into my pocket and pulled out another bill. Cocky saw the money and something bright and eager crept into his expression. He looked at the twenty the same way a drunk eyes a fifth of booze. If he'd been a dog, he'd be drooling.

I said, "Tell me about Caballos."

Cocky kept his eyes on the money, probably calculating the odds of pulling off a snatch and grab. "He's nobody," he finally said.

"I heard he's got a direct line to Harper."

"You want Harper, I can deliver Harper just as good as this other guy. He don't got nothin' on me. You work with me an' I'll set you up with anybody you say."

"I don't want to be set up. Tell me what you know about Caballos."

"Forget Caballos. Go with me. I'm yer guy."

"Ask around," I said, and stuffed the money into his pocket. "Discreetly. That means don't mention my name, understand? If this comes back to me, I swear I'll come and get you where you live, Cocky."

I released his arm and left him staring after me as I walked back to Blackie's car.

"Where'd you pick up that slime-fuck?" Blackie asked as I slid into the passenger seat beside him.

"Parole," I said. "He's straight now. Sells confessions to the cops."

Blackie scowled and reached for a cigarette. "Nothing like a government rat for integrity."

I watched Cocky Burnett meander down the street, then cross to the Hall of Justice side. He stopped near the foot of the stairs and propped himself against a parked car. Then he pulled out a toothpick and glanced over his shoulder at me. Blackie swore.

"He's going to ask around about Caballos," I said.

Blackie used a match to light his cigarette, then tossed the match into the rumble of trash at our feet. I half expected the whole mess to go up in flames every time he did it, but so far his luck had held.

"Can't trust a snitch, doll. You know that."

I did. But I'd made the call and I had to go with it. Maybe, just maybe, Cocky Burnett wouldn't turn on me. I'd given him more breaks than he'd ever deserved when I was his parole officer and against all my experience I hoped that would make a difference if it came to screwing me over.

Blackie rolled his window down to let the smoke out of the car, then glanced over at the

Hall of Justice and said, "How'd you do up there? Anything?"

I told him again about the college-professor theory and how I'd set it up to go show the picture around. He squinted at me and said, "Fuck. You working for Post now?"

"He doesn't know anything about it."

Blackie said something, but I didn't catch it. I was too busy checking out a stocky, arrogant-looking man strolling hurriedly down the street. "Speaking of," I said. "There's Harper now."

Blackie followed my gaze, then chuckled with satisfaction. "Looks pissed."

Harper's eyes flickered when he walked past Cocky Burnett. That was the only sign that the two men knew each other, but Blackie and I both caught it.

"Shit," I said. I shouldn't have mentioned Caballos's name. Or Harper's.

When Harper reached the stairs, he slowed and took them with dignity, like a king ascending his throne. Cocky Burnett glanced over his shoulder in my direction, touched two fingers to his temple in a not-too-surreptitious salute, and scurried up the stairs in time to open the door for Harper.

Once they'd vanished inside, I turned to Blackie. "Does Harper look like a bad guy to you?"

"Fuck." Blackie reached for the ignition and cranked the engine. "These days, who doesn't?"

28

The call came later in the afternoon when I was sitting around waiting to hear from Checker. Instead of the fat detective's raspy, slightly out-of-breath voice, the one on the line was deeply melodic and Latin.

"Señorita Ventana? Lucho Navarro."

It took me a minute to remember. He was the neighborhood-watch guy, the one who'd known my dad.

"Are you free, señorita? Can you come to El Gallo Prieto now?"

"Well, I—"

"There is someone here that perhaps you should speak to."

"Look, Mr. Navarro. I'm not big in the suspense department."

"It is someone who may be of assistance to you in your *investigación*. Please. It is best to be discreet, no? It would be an honor to make a contribution."

I made it to El Gallo Prieto bar on Valencia in twenty minutes, thinking the whole time that I was making a big mistake. The place was packed, even though it was only four in the afternoon, and the mariachi music on the jukebox was enough to make Linda Ronstadt swoon.

"Ah, Señorita Ventana," Lucho Navarro said when he'd cut his way through the crowd to meet me at the bar. He smiled, and his white teeth gleamed in stark contrast to his swarthy skin and the deep-black droop of his Pancho Villa mustache. He looked younger than he had the other night, fifty, maybe, instead of sixty, with just the slightest touch of gray around his otherwise black-as-night hair.

I nodded in greeting, then said, "You've got something?"

"Downstairs," he said, so I followed him down a narrow flight of steps into a well-lit basement. There were tidy stacks of boxes—paper napkins, beer, and hard booze—filling most of the space, but it didn't look cluttered. I followed Navarro to a narrow door under the stairs. He opened it and stepped inside, saying, "Hombres, sorry to keep you waiting but we are here now."

The room was small and cramped, with a bare bulb dangling from a wire that vanished into a hole in the ceiling. Two dark-haired Mexican men—really one man and a cherub-faced teenager with an aura of black curls—sat on folding chairs at a card table. The man looked placid, amiable even, but the kid was sulking. It was pretty obvious he didn't want to be there.

Except for two empty beer bottles, the table was empty.

Navarro pulled over a third chair, asked me to sit, then got one for himself. "This is Angel," he said, indicating the older man. "And this is his grandson, Manolo."

Navarro turned to the sullen boy. "Tell her, Manolo."

The kid, who couldn't have been more than sixteen, stared at me with contempt. Maybe he thought he had to act tough because the face he'd been born with looked, even through the sullenness, as angelic and sweet as an altar boy's. Or maybe he'd had his cheeks pinched one time too many.

I stared right back at him, hard, until he blinked and looked away. Beside me the corners of Navarro's mustache lifted slightly.

"We don't have to be friends," I said to the kid. "You don't even have to like me. Just say what you've got to say."

The kid raised his eyes. There was surprise in them. And some of the tough act was gone.

"He knows about Caballos," the older man said, and jabbed the kid's shoulder with a couple of stiff fingers. "*Habla, mijo.*"

The boy sat, sullen and silent.

"Perhaps another *cerveza* will loosen his tongue," Navarro said.

The older man went upstairs, then came down clutching four beer bottles by their necks. The one he set before the boy was nonalcoholic.

"So what about Caballos?" I asked, trying not to choke on the dead man's name.

The kid swigged his fake beer and seemed to relax a little. He glanced around the room, like he was trying to reassure himself there was no other way out of this. Then finally he spoke. His voice was surprisingly deep.

"You want to know about Caballos? He's the bro'-in-law's partner, man. They been runnin' together, hangin' real tight the last couple of months, since my bro'-in-law came home."

Nothing about a dead Caballos. "Where's he been, this brother-in-law?"

"The Q." San Quentin.

"What's your brother-in-law's name?"

The kid's dark eyes flitted over to Navarro, who nodded imperceptibly, then back to me. "Valentín. Valentín Garcia."

"What was he in for?"

The kid hesitated again. "I thought you wanted to know about Caballos."

The old man shot him a dirty look.

"Ever hear that saying, Tell me who you walk with and I'll tell you who you are?" I said.

From his expression it was obvious he hadn't.

"Forget it," I said. "What about Caballos?"

"He's into a lot of stuff, man, but mostly he's gettin' a rep around cars. Any kinda car you want, he gets it. You—say you want a red Beemer? You got it like *that*—" He snapped his fingers. "In a day. Ferrari, Lexus, anything you want, he can get it. The bro'-in-law's ride's a brand-new silver Beem. Cost him three C's, man."

"Have you heard anything about Caballos selling information?"

The kid blinked, then smiled. "You mean like a snitch?"

I nodded.

"Nah. The bro' wouldn't hang with no snitch."

I looked the kid over. Cherub face, pouting lips. "You don't like Caballos?"

The kid blinked again. "What makes you think I don't like him? I didn't say that."

"You're talking to me about him, aren't you?"

The kid started to protest, but the man sitting next to him interrupted. "Caballos wanted to pimp the boy," he said, then sat there and seethed.

I glanced at Navarro, mostly so the kid wouldn't feel like I was staring at him. Navarro said, "Angel is the boy's grandfather."

I listened while Angel told how the kid had come to him, terrified after Caballos had offered him five hundred dollars to get friendly with a certain city supervisor.

"Are you sure it was a supervisor? Could it have been a D.A.?"

"He said 'supervisor,' but *coño*, not for any amount of money would I do that," the kid said, blushing and finally looking and acting his age. "I'm no *maricón*."

"Think he really meant it?"

The kid acted insulted. "He showed me the money, man. It was for real."

"Ever heard of Arnaldo Contreras?"

•

"No."

The grandfather shook his head when I arched my brow at him.

I was starting to think the trip hadn't been worth it, then I remembered the missing fat man. According to Marina, Caballos had been with a fat, sweaty man the night he'd dumped the body on Sunset. I looked across the table at the kid.

"Tell me about your brother-in-law. What's he look like?"

The kid scowled. "I thought you wanted to know about Caballos. They only been running dogs a couple of months, man. It's not like they're blood or nothin'."

"Is your brother-in-law fat?"

"Valentín? Nah. The food's no good at the Q. He lost seventeen pounds, man. He's all bones now, an' my sister and his mom's workin' hard all day in the kitchen to put it back on."

"Did Valentín and Caballos meet in San Quentin?"

The boy shook his head and his curls moved in a wave. "This *'mano* who was in the Q with Valentín, they got their freedom on the same day. I guess he knew Caballos from before, 'cause he hooked 'em up together, you know, the next week, and Valentín got his car. That's how they met, over the car."

"What's that guy's name?" I asked.

"Silvio Gutierrez. But everybody calls him *El Gordo*," the kid said.

El Gordo. The Fat Man.

29

El Gordo lived in a little shack behind a warehouse off Folsom Street. In the misty morning light the place didn't look as bad as it might have under the harsh glare of the noon sun, but it still looked pretty shabby.

"Just 'cause the lights are on doesn't mean he's going to come out," Marina said.

She'd been acting weird and grumpy all morning. Instead of being happy to skip school when I had shown up at her front door this morning, she'd said she had an important class she couldn't miss.

"You're going to turn this down for a math class? It's real P.I. work."

She shrugged.

"It's what you've always wanted, Marina."

She stared at her shoes, then raised her eyes to look past my shoulder out the door to my car. "I know."

"So?"

"So I got this class."

She wouldn't look me in the eye.

"Hey, you want to talk about it?"

"About what?"

"About what's bothering you?"

"Nothing's bothering me."

"Is it Caballos? Are you still worried about him?"

She sort of flinched and I took that to mean she was.

"Hey, Marina. Look at me."

She kept her eyes on the scuffed-up floor.

"I told you you don't have to worry about that guy and I mean it. Okay? Are we clear here? There's no way he's going to hurt you."

"Nothing's botherin' me." She gathered her books off the little hall table and hugged them to her flat chest. "I gotta go."

"Wait. Marina. *Please.* I need your help on this. You're the only one who can I.D. this fat man."

She slung her books from one arm to the other and looked peeved. "Why should I? It won't make any difference anyway. They don't believe me. I'll just get into more trouble."

"Is that it? Is that the holdup? Listen, you're not doing this for the police, Marina. This is for me. *I'm* working this thing."

She came along then, but she'd been quiet and distant and different. And now that we'd spent the last two hours sitting in silence in my cramped little '77 Toyota, even the tiniest spark of her reluctant enthusiasm had vanished.

"I bet he's never going to come out," she muttered. "What if they told him?"

She was talking about the kid and his grandfather.

"They didn't warn him," I said. "Navarro vouched for them and Navarro's good for his word."

"How do you know?"

"I trust the guy. What if I gave you my word on something? Wouldn't you trust me on it?"

She looked stricken.

"Well? Wouldn't you?"

"Sure. But—"

"It's the same deal—I know about Navarro like you know about me."

She stared sullenly out the window and after a while said, "You ever kill somebody?"

"No."

"Think you ever will?"

"I don't know. I'd like to think I won't, but I don't know. I'd probably try to figure out some way to avoid it if I could."

"My uncle killed people."

"I know. For money. That was his choice. He went looking for it."

She turned again and stared out the window some more until a movement at the little shack caught my eye.

"Heads up," I said.

The door opened and somebody stepped out. Beside me Marina tensed.

"Is that him?" I asked.

A fat man waddled out to a parked car a

couple of doors down from the shack and heaved his bulk into the driver's seat. He was built like Santa Claus with a beardless face as round as the moon. Thick cords of oily black hair hung uncombed from his head and he looked like he'd slept in his faded overalls and flannel shirt for at least a week. You could almost see the aroma waft off him.

"Is that the guy, Marina?"

"That's him," she whispered. "He's the one."

The Fat Man wedged himself into the driver's seat of an antique Chevy, slammed the door shut, and tried for about three minutes without any luck to get it to start. He finally gave up, heaved himself out of the car, and lumbered off down the alley toward Mission. I let him vanish around the corner, then turned the engine in the Toyota.

"What are we going to do now?" Marina asked. She looked terrified. Her breathing had quickened and her eyes were wide. Her voice quivered. "Are we going to follow him?"

I glanced over at her and considered it. If she stayed in the car, maybe it would be all right. "Promise you'll do exactly what I tell you to do."

"Are you going to kill him? Do you have a gun?"

"I don't need a gun. Just promise you'll do what I tell you."

"What do you want me to do?"

"I don't know yet."

We ended up trailing him for a couple of blocks down Mission while Marina chattered excitedly—partly from fear, no doubt. Then I pulled to the curb and shut off the engine.

"Stay here," I said, and jumped out before she could object.

By the time I caught up to El Gordo, he was another block farther down crowded Mission Street. He was sweating, from the walking, I guess, and he had really bad body odor, just like I thought he would.

"Excuse me," I said when I came abreast of him.

He glanced over at me with tiny piglike eyes.

"Yeah?" He didn't lose momentum, he just kept barging through the throng of late-morning shoppers. Somebody bumped my shoulder and I had to take a couple of double steps to catch back up to him.

"You don't know me," I began. "But we've got a mutual acquaintance."

He kept walking, but glanced over his shoulder to see if there was anybody with me. He checked out the people across the street, then brought his eyes back to me. "Yeah?"

This guy probably killed people for a living, because he was too rude to ever hold down a real job.

"Ever heard of Herbie Caballos?" I asked pleasantly.

He kept moving. "Never heard of the guy."

"Maybe you know him by his alias—Have you heard of Arnaldo Contreras?"

"Get lost."

"I guess you won't be going to his funeral, then."

He stopped dead in the middle of the sidewalk, slack-jawed with surprise, and blinked. A woman pushing a stroller behind us rammed into him from the back.

"Watch it," he snarled, then turned back to me. "What did you just say?"

"I didn't think you knew him."

"Cut the crap, lady. What kind of shakedown you running?"

"No shakedown."

People were swarming past us, giving us annoyed side glances because we weren't moving. The Fat Man didn't even notice.

"Is this supposed to be some kind of joke?" he said.

"You're not laughing. I'm not laughing. Draw your own conclusion."

His tiny eyes narrowed. "Who are you? What do you want?"

"Think of me as somebody you need to level with."

"Why should I?"

"Because it beats leveling with the police."

"How do I know *you're* not the law?"

"Because you'd already be in the back of a squad car on your way to the Hall of Justice. But I guess that could change. I mean, if they got a tip, who knows?"

He frowned.

I said, "Tell me about Arnaldo Contreras."

"Never heard of him."

"Just like you never heard of Herbie?"

"They already talked to Herbie. They let him go. They're looking some place else."

"That was before Herbie died. They might think things deserve a second look now, with Herbie gone and all."

He glared at me. "What do you want?"

"Tell me about that corpse you and Herbie dumped out on Sunset Boulevard."

He turned away and started walking fast back the way he'd come. I followed him. "Just tell me the dead guy's name. Who was he? Why did you kill him?"

"Man, I don't know nothing about that."

"Sure you do. I've got a witness who saw you there."

"The kid? The kid's bullshit."

"Where does Harland Harper fit in? Did he hire you and Herbie?"

He stopped suddenly. "Harper? The guy's runnin' for mayor?" He looked puzzled, then suddenly alarmed. "You gotta be kiddin' me."

"What was his name? Why did Harper want him dead?"

Instead of answering, his eyes went inward, like he didn't even see me anymore. That's when I realized he didn't know.

"Tell me about Herbie," I said. "How did you connect with him? You can tell me or you can tell the cops."

As soon as I spoke, his attention snapped back to the present. He looked up and down the street, then said, "I got a better idea."

Before I knew what had happened, he grabbed my throat and slammed me up against the side of a parked van. He stuck his face up close to mine, so close I could see tiny bubbles of spittle on his teeth when he spoke. I could make out the little papillae on his tongue. All around us people scattered.

"You leave me out of this," he whispered hoarsely. His rancid-smelling breath felt hot and damp on my face. "You forget you ever saw me or you're going to be real sorry. Understand?"

"Aaack!" I gasped for air and clawed at his hand, but his fingers were like a vise on my throat.

"Understand?" His fingers tightened down some more and he gave my neck a little shake.

I tried to say yes, but there just wasn't any air left inside me. Big black spots were starting to close in, and things were going dark. Then, from nowhere, I heard a shout and something rushed at us.

It was Marina, wielding an umbrella—the umbrella I always keep in a pile of junk on the backseat of my car. She clubbed the Fat Man on the back of his head with the handle, then drew back and jabbed him in the ribs.

"Aaargh!" he shouted, then dropped his hands from my throat and turned toward Marina.

"Run!" she shouted, crying and dancing around like the sidewalk was made of hot coals.

But all I could do was sort of stumble around and gasp for air. People had pretty much cleared the area, so I didn't bump into anybody, but I wish I had. I took in a couple of good, deep breaths, and things started to crystallize. Marina was backing away from El Gordo, sobbing and jabbing, and shouting at me.

"Run, Ronnie! Run!"

She jabbed at him again and he grabbed the umbrella and yanked it toward him. Marina let go just in time, then skittered back, inches out of his reach.

One last breath cleared my head. I circled the Fat Man and shoved Marina toward the car.

"Let's go," I said as I sprinted with her down the street. I glanced over my shoulder and grinned when I saw her puffing behind me. And the Fat Man, the Fat Man stood like a greasy lump on the sidewalk, snowshoe-sized feet planted firmly, clutching the umbrella and staring after us with an angry but puzzled look on his face.

"We got him!" Marina shouted elatedly as we dove into the Toyota. I cranked the engine, made a U-turn in the middle of Mission, and floored it. Beside me, Marina tried to catch her breath.

"Thanks," I said once we'd hit South Van Ness.

Marina giggled deliriously. The exhilaration put a wild cast in her eyes I'd never seen before. "That was awful," she announced breathlessly.

I touched my still-smarting throat. "You're right."

"All those stupid people just standing around! Not doing anything! One *pendejo* even tried to hold me back. I can't believe nobody wanted to help you. And nobody wanted me to help you either."

"That's life," I said.

"Don't you wish you had a gun?"

"That guy's no good to me dead."

"He was trying to *kill* you."

"He didn't, though. And if I'd killed him, I'd probably go to jail and for sure not know what any of this is all about." Morality 101 for the niece of a contract killer.

"Did he tell you?"

"Not exactly. But I found out we don't need to bother with him anymore."

"Why? Are you going to let him scare you off like that?" Marina didn't bother to hide her scorn.

"He's just hired muscle, Marina. He doesn't matter. He wasn't really in on the deal except maybe to make a couple of bucks. Nobody told him anything, so he couldn't tell us anything even if he wanted to. Believe me, that guy's in the dark."

Marina looked relieved. I guess she was happy she wouldn't have to think of me as a chicken-hearted dummy. I was happy about that too.

I stopped at a red light, and Marina asked, "What are we going to do now?"

"You're going back to school."

She wailed out a string of protests, which I ignored.

"What are *you* going to do?" she finally asked when she realized I wasn't going to budge.

I thought about where things stood: The Fat

Man was a zero, a dead end. Caballos alias Contreras was a dead end for now too. I could work the trail on Harland Harper. Or I could go at it from the John Doe. Maybe, just maybe, I could coax the dead man to speak.

30

It was cruel to expect Marina to sit through a biology lecture after something like that, but I dropped her off at Mission High anyway, with a warning to keep her eyes open and to travel in packs if she went out at night. El Gordo was probably halfway to Fresno by now, but it never hurt to be wary.

When I reached the Hall of Justice, I was glad to find Checker alone at his desk. No partner and no Philly Post in sight. I'd called ahead and told him I was on my way over to pick up the photograph of the John Doe so maybe he'd cleared them out with some phony-baloney excuse.

Whatever the deal was, he was being so nice and cooperative about it, I felt a twinge of guilt over not telling him that Caballos was dead and that I'd found El Gordo. But it was just a twinge and it went away real fast.

"Here's what we got," Checker said, holding the photograph in his hand and staring down at it. I waited for him to hand it to me, but he didn't.

"This isn't how we usually do business," he said.

"Me, neither."

"Huh?"

"I usually don't offer my services for free."

Checker frowned, and all the frumpy kindness left his face. He looked suddenly tired, tired and disgusted. "Are you trying to tell me you want to get paid for doing this?"

"I'm not saying that at all."

"Well, good. 'Cause the whole reason we're even agreeing to let you in on this thing boils down to budget. Me and Marks are carrying extra caseload 'cause we got a head-count freeze on the department. Marks, he doesn't think it's such a great idea. He put a condition on it."

I waited.

"It's like this: You work directly with us. You find something—anything, you bring it to us. Nobody else."

"Nobody? You mean nobody like Philly Post?"

He sort of blanched.

"Don't worry," I said, extending my hand for the picture. "I won't tell if you won't."

He held on to the photograph. "It's just that we're really swamped right now. Otherwise we'd never even consider it. I've never seen so much happen at once, and I've been with the P.D. for fifteen years."

I waited.

"There's one more thing."

I sighed. This was turning out to be more complicated than I thought. He was probably going to ask me to sign something in blood next.

"If you get a hit—"

"I bring it to you. Yeah, I got that part."

"Okay, if you get a hit, you bring it to us. And that's it. You're out of it."

Leave it to a bunch of bureaucrats to fret over who's going to get the credit. "Don't worry. It'll be our little secret."

Downstairs, while I waited for one of the pay phones to open up, I pulled the Polaroid out of the envelope Checkers had put it in. The picture was pretty bad—not quality-wise but aesthetics-wise. You'd have to be pretty dumb or pretty blind not to notice the guy was dead. His skin was gray, his eyes were shut, and every muscle in his face was as relaxed as putty. *Rigor mortis* had come and gone. Great.

Something nudged my elbow. I looked up from the picture and found a black stringbean of a guy in a leather jacket and big, pleading eyes.

"You waitin' on the phone?" he asked.

I followed his gaze to the empty kiosk. "Thanks."

I went over and rifled through the phone book until I found "Schools-Academic-Colleges & Universities." Then I tore the page out, folded it, and stuck it into my pocket as I walked out of the building into the golden afternoon sunlight.

31

"Is this guy sick?" the personnel secretary at Golden Gate University asked when I showed her the picture.

"Do you know him?"

She made a face and handed the photo back. "Our faculty's usually a little more animated than that."

Nobody knew him at Hastings, UCSF, or UC Extension Center either. I tried the University of San Francisco without any luck, then gave up on four-year higher education and headed south to City College.

"I'm new here," the fresh-faced kid at the front desk said.

I glanced around the office. Nobody looked over the age of twelve. "Who isn't?"

"Try Lainie. Over there."

I crossed the hall and went into another office filled with computers and more twelve-year-olds.

"Lainie?" I called out.

A slender black man looked up from behind one of the computers and smiled. "Over here."

I wound my way through the desks over to his and pulled up an empty chair.

"Hi," he said, punching a few last keys on the keyboard, then turning to me. "What can I do for you?"

I pulled out the Polaroid and set it on the table next to the keyboard. "I'm trying to locate this man," I said. "He might be a teacher here."

"May I?" Lainie reached for the photo.

He studied it, then frowned. "He doesn't look so good."

"Do you know him?"

"His name's Sam Ackerman. Is he okay? I've never seen him look like that."

"Is he a teacher here?"

"I wish. This guy's one of the best journalists in the world."

The name finally clicked. "*That* Sam Ackerman?"

Lainie ticked accomplishments off on his fingers: Investigative reporter. Exposé of a southern California prison warden running drug deals out of his office. A critically acclaimed analysis and coverage of the rise of tuberculosis in the homeless community of San Francisco. A book critical of the state's environmental policies.

"Didn't he win a Pulitzer?"

"That's the one. He works at the *Chronicle*."

I stared at the image of the innocuous-looking dead guy in the photograph. Why hadn't anybody reported him missing? "Are you sure?"

"I'll never forget him. He guest-lectured here one day and he had all the students in the lecture hall on their feet cheering by the time he was finished. And all the four-year colleges were jumping up and down demanding to know why he wouldn't do them too. You know what he said? This was great: He said the big four-year colleges don't need him, we do."

Lainie tapped the picture with his index finger, and his smile broadened. "I'd know this guy anywhere. He's got class."

I found a pay phone outside the campus bookstore, dropped a pair of dimes into it, and stopped. This was where I was supposed to call Checker and Marks and tell them what I had.

I thought about the two of them, slogging methodically through the mountains of paperwork on their desks like two old dying buffalo working their way west, and dialed up the *Chronicle* instead.

"Sam Ackerman, please."

"He's on a leave of absence, miss. Is there someone else you'd like to speak to instead?"

"For how long?"

"Sorry?"

"How long is he expected to be on leave?"

"I'm not sure, miss."

"Then let me talk to his boss."

"Mr. Ackerman reports directly to the

publisher, miss. Do you wish to speak to Mr. Cavanaugh?"

But Mr. Ira Cavanaugh's secretary—only she called herself his executive assistant—turned out to be the human equivalent of a snarling pit bull. I tried every excuse in the world and still couldn't get through. Finally I hung up, waited five minutes, and called back.

Using a much deeper voice and slower phrasing, I said, "Mr. Cavanaugh, please. This is his CPA's office calling."

"Mr. Landry always handles Mr. Cavanaugh's taxes. Who are you?"

"I'm Mr. Landry's new partner. Mr. Landry's vacationing in Ethiopia right now, but this is sort of an emergency."

"An emergency? What sort of emergency? What is this regarding?"

"The I.R.S. called. They're contemplating an audit and they're not going to wait for Mr. Landry to get back to make up their minds. Unless I speak with Mr. Cavanaugh right now about his schedules C, D, E, F, and G, we may not be able to avoid it."

There was a long pause on the other end. I could hear her exhale in a long drawn-out sigh. Finally she said, "Very well, then. I'll put you through. One moment, please."

A split second later a richly resonant voice said, "Ike Cavanaugh here. What's up?"

"I'm calling about Sam Ackerman, Mr. Cavanaugh. I understand he's on a leave of absence. Is that right?"

There was a long silence. "Ackerman? You're not the accountant?"

"No. Your secretary must have misunderstood. Sam's on leave?"

"That's right," he said, and his voice warmed like a doting father's. "Been gone for a couple of weeks now. Who'd you say you were?"

"I'm his second cousin and I'm in town from Nevada for a month. Haven't had any luck reaching him at home. Is he working on another Pulitzer?"

Cavanaugh's chuckle was hearty. "That's the idea. If you want to get in touch with Sam, try calling back every other week. He'll probably come up for air sometime."

"Have you talked to him lately?"

"Not a chance. You know Sam, he starts in on a story and nobody hears from him for weeks at a time. My other reporters all want to know why they can't have the same latitude I give Sam. I tell them they can soon as they bring home a Pulitzer. Sam does a lot of undercover, you know."

"What's he working on, do you know?"

Cavanaugh laughed again. "If I did, you can believe I wouldn't tell a complete stranger on the telephone. Sam always plays it pretty close to the vest. He likes to surprise me."

"You don't know what he's working on?"

"No."

"Could it be dangerous?"

"Could be," he answered cheerily.

"Do you know if it involves Harland Harper?"

"Haven't a clue. I never do. And he's never disappointed me. The only thing I can tell you, and this is a direct quote from Sam: This story's going to shatter rock when it hits the streets."

32

I dropped another pair of dimes into the pay phone and called my contact at the phone company to trade jazzing up his burglar alarm—the one I'd put in for him last year—for both Ackerman's unlisted home number and his address. Then I dialed the number and listened while his answering machine picked up.

"This is Sam," the tape-recorded voice said. "I'll call you back when I can."

I hung up the phone and stared out across the City College campus. I hadn't thought hearing Sam Ackerman's voice would affect me much, but it did. It was warm and deep and resonated with kindness. It matched his face—not the one in the photograph I'd been showing around but the one I'd seen Tuesday night, the night he'd died. I thought about that night and felt suddenly overwhelmed with sadness.

What's your story, Sam? I thought as I watched the quickly gathering dusk. *What's your story? And why did Herbie and the Fat Man kill for it?*

33

I did what usually always works for me when I need to clear my head—I went home, slipped into a T-shirt, shorts, and running shoes, and headed for the Golden Gate Bridge. I ran down Columbus to Bay, then through Fort Mason and the Marina Green and on to Crissy Field.

It was my second run of the day, but I needed it and it felt good. I ran, sucking in deep breaths of the foggy evening air, letting the wind cool my skin as it dried my perspiration. I measured my pace and kept my mind free of everything but the consoling rhythm of my footfalls. And by the time I got home an hour later, it was nearly dusk. I felt, if not happy and carefree, at least cleansed.

When I passed the Quarter Moon on the way to my apartment, Blackie lurched out the door clutching a crumpled evening newspaper in his big boxer's fist.

"Hey, doll."

I was going to crack a joke, then took one look at his face and said, "What's wrong?"

His sexy blue eyes bored into mine. He touched my elbow and nodded toward my building. "Let's take it inside."

We climbed the steps in silence and Blackie waited solemnly while I unlocked the door and led him into my one-room apartment.

"What is it?" I said once he'd closed the door behind us.

Blackie's voice was gruff. "You leave any prints on that van?"

"What van?"

"The one with the stiff in it, doll. You had gloves, right?"

"Yes. What's this about?"

"Bad news, doll. Real bad. You better hope nobody saw us ransacking that shit."

"What are you talking about?"

He rubbed the back of his neck without answering.

"*Blackie.*"

"The stiff?" he said.

"Right. Herbie Caballos, alias Arnaldo Contreras. What about him?"

I'd forgotten about the crumpled newspaper in his hand, but now Blackie shoved it toward me.

"Read it and weep, doll. Fucker was an undercover cop."

34

"What do you mean?"

"He was a fuckin' cop. The big dogs'll be comin' out for this one, doll."

I stared blindly down at the newspaper in my hand and tried to think. He was a policeman. He worked for the *police*. That was why nobody believed Marina. That was why he had Harland Harper's beeper number. But it didn't explain why he killed Sam Ackerman.

"Here." Blackie reached over and pointed to a little square at the bottom of the page.

POLICEMAN FOUND SHOT. Three sentences described the dead man and where he'd been found. His name was Pedro Rubio.

"It's all over the news—TV, radio," Blackie said. "They're not saying what he was workin', but they ran a picture of the van on the five o'clock news."

At the mention of the van, the vividly gory picture of Pedro Rubio's splattered brains popped into my mind. Then I remembered the back of the van. I folded the newspaper and shoved it into Blackie's hands. "The box of stuff we took—what happened to it?"

"I took care of it."

"You destroyed it?"

Blackie scowled. "It's in Joey's basement."

Blackie's son, Joey, had so much junk in his basement, he'd never notice one more box. It would be safe there.

"Things get hot, I got a pal down the block from Joey's with an incinerator behind his store. He's all right—no questions, ever."

I tossed the newspaper onto the couch and crossed the room. "This means we've got to do it tonight."

From behind me, as I threw open the closet and started rummaging through the dirty clothes piled on the floor, Blackie asked, "Do what?"

"Break in to Sam Ackerman's house."

I found the black jeans I was looking for, sniffed them, and decided they weren't too ripe to wear one more time. My black sweatshirt was on the shelf just inside the closet door. I grabbed it and stepped back into the room.

Blackie hadn't moved. He was lighting a cigarette and giving me the fish eye.

"Who the fuck is Sam Ackerman?"

Clutching my clothes in one hand, I crossed the room and pulled the photograph out from under the phone book. I'd put it there before I went out to run because I didn't want to come home and have to look at it. I glimpsed his sad, dead face now as I handed it to Blackie.

"Sam Ackerman," I said, and some of the grief I'd felt earlier welled up inside me again. I cleared my throat. "Ace reporter. Pulitzer prizewinner. Our former John Doe. The one Marina says the undercover cop killed. Are you up for it?"

"The chubby cops know?"

"Not yet." I jingled my bag of burglar tools and grinned. "What do you say?"

Blackie tossed the snapshot onto the table and exhaled a cloud of smoke into the room. With a scowl he said, "Like I got a fuckin' choice."

35

eside me, Blackie rolled down his old Buick's window and flicked his cigarette butt in an arc through the darkness. We were parked up the block from Ackerman's little cottage on De Haro Street in Potrero Hill. There was a liquor store a couple of doors down from the eight-foot-high, ivy-topped solid wood fence that stretched across Ackerman's front yard. The fence was solid except for some space left open high on either side of the arched gate.

"You sure you wanna do this?" Blackie asked.

"We don't have a choice, Blackie. Once the police find out their John Doe is Sam Ackerman, they're going to be all over this place."

"What makes you think they haven't already?"

I grinned. "Blind hope?"

Blackie cursed.

"Checker and Marks would never have given me that picture if they had even the remotest clue who this guy was."

"A lotta water under the bridge since this morning, doll."

"Don't remind me."

"Wanna work the lock on the gate or go in over the fence?" Blackie asked.

I watched the steady stream of people passing by on the sidewalk in front of Ackerman's gate. They all seemed pretty intent on making it to the store for their evening fifth, and none of them looked like they enjoyed a real solid relationship with the police. But you can never tell.

"Too many people around to risk going over," I said, slipping on a pair of gloves and handing a second set to Blackie. "They might not call it in, but they might try to shake us down when we come back out."

Blackie reached under his seat and pulled out a crowbar. "Gimme five minutes and I'll convince 'em *that's* a bad idea."

"Maybe."

I ended up picking the lock, which was quick and simple, because Ackerman hadn't spent a lot of money on it. It might not be true about much these days, but with locks you can pretty much bet that you get what you pay for.

Blackie and I were inside the gate within seconds. As soon as the latch clicked shut behind us, I blinked to adjust my eyes to the darkness. A wild natural garden bordered either side of the stairs that wound uphill toward a tiny cottage at the high back end of the lot. Blackie followed me up the path to the deck, then kept watch behind us as I rang the doorbell.

I was ready with my oh-the-front-gate-wasn't-latched spiel in case anybody answered, but I didn't need it. Nobody came to the door. And from the little I could see of the neighbors' houses, nobody was home next door either.

Picking the front-door lock took a little longer—he'd sprung for a higher-class rig here—but we were inside with no real sweat. Blackie went automatically to the windows and pulled the drapes while I looked around.

The living room was small, but he'd managed to make it comfortable with a couple of armchairs, a television in one corner, and a desk and a computer in another. The softwood floors were bare and, after I'd had a good look around, so was the rest of the house. Either Sam Ackerman was a neat freak or somebody had cleaned him out.

Sure, his neatly pressed clothes hung in the closet, and there was food in the fridge and in the kitchen cabinets, but there was none of the usual stuff that fills a house when somebody lives in it—no books, no magazines, no newspapers (which was really weird for a journalist), no letters, no bills, nothing—just food and furniture. Except for the computer there was nothing else on his desk or in the drawers.

I reached around to the back of the computer and switched it on. The screen came up blank. I fiddled with it but couldn't get it to do anything. Blackie came up behind me.

"Whatcha got, doll?"

"Nothing. Somebody erased our guy's files. This thing's as empty as the day he bought it."

Blackie flashed his tiny penlight around the empty desk drawers. "Cleaned the fucker out, huh?"

"Let's go over the place one more time."

I rose and went to the bedroom. The phone answering machine on the nightstand next to the bed still had the greeting tape, the one you hear when you call in, but the second tape, the one that recorded incoming messages, was missing.

The closet was filled with clothes and so was the chest of drawers, but there wasn't a single scrap of paper anywhere. Same with the bathroom. Same with the kitchen—not even a shopping list.

I went back to the kitchen, opened one of the kitchen cabinets and stood staring at its contents. Seventeen packages of chicken-flavored instant soup. Pancake mix. Three cans of vegetarian refried beans. Two sacks of tortilla chips. Two jars of Gatorade. And two boxes of Cheerios, both opened.

I picked up the first one and looked inside. Cheerios. I stuck my hand inside and felt around. Nothing but cereal. But I had to be sure. I hurriedly spread a couple of paper towels out on the counter and poured out the contents of the box just as Blackie stepped into the room.

"Hungry?" he asked with a grin.

"I'm looking for secret hiding places. Want to check the fridge?"

He took a step, then froze. "You been out back yet?" he asked.

I stopped stuffing the Cheerios back into the box and followed his gaze. The back door was ajar, just slightly, but definitely open. I'd seen it on my first pass through. "The pry marks don't look that fresh," I said. "Go ahead and check the yard in case I'm wrong."

Blackie pulled his crowbar out of his duffel and disappeared into the dark. I finished stuffing the Cheerios back into the box, set it on the shelf and, keeping an eye on the back door, reached for the second box. It felt different—heavier— than the first one. I shook it, then opened it and looked inside. There were documents and papers folded neatly inside its wax-paper liner.

Blackie appeared at the door. "There's a basement downstairs. Nothing in it but firewood."

I tucked the cereal box under my arm and went to the fridge. The butter was real butter and the carton of milk was really milk—really sour milk. I took one last sweeping glance around the room, then said, "Come on, Blackie, our time's up. Let's go."

Down at the gate, just inside the wooden fence, the moonlight glinted off something metallic. It looked like a metal box nailed at chest level to the fence. "Wait up, Blackie."

I stepped off the path for a closer look in the dusky light. It was a mailbox fashioned from an old tackle box. It should have been overflowing with mail, but it wasn't. Blackie made some sort of urgent sound behind me.

"Coming," I whispered. I lifted the lid. There were a couple of magazines and three envelopes inside. I grabbed them all, stuffed them into the Cheerios box, hugged it to my chest, and scurried out into the street after Blackie.

26

I had noticed the brown sedan parked at the corner of Grant Avenue and decided to ignore it, but then its door swung open and Philly Post popped out. He reached me and Blackie just as I stood on the stoop unlocking my building's front door.

"Fuck," Blackie muttered with a glance over his shoulder. "Thought I smelled somethin' bad."

"Shut up, Coogan." Post's eyes flickered over the box of Cheerios in my hand. "Dressed kind of shady for a trip to the supermarket, aren't you, Ventana?"

I offered him a dour smile. "Is this a social call, Lieutenant, or are you working for the fashion police now?"

He started to scowl, then checked himself. He motioned toward the half-open door. "Can we talk upstairs?"

"About what?"

"The kid."

"What kid?"

"The Murieta kid."

My heart quickened. "What about her? Is she okay?"

"Can we go upstairs?"

I searched his unreadable face. "Is she okay?" I asked again.

Post stared at me, and when I didn't back down, he seemed, for the moment, to give up trying to get upstairs. "We want to talk to her, that's all."

"Have you tried her house?"

"She's gone, Ventana." He glanced up at my darkened window. "But then you probably already knew that."

"How could I? What do you mean 'gone'?"

" 'Gone' as in 'absent,' Ventana." He nudged his way closer to the door.

"She's not here," I said.

"Mind if I come up and see for myself?"

"Yes."

Post glanced at Blackie, then back at me. His jaw tightened. "I can get a warrant."

"So get one."

Blackie stepped in front of the half-opened door, but Post ignored him.

"You sayin' you don't know where she is?" he asked.

"That's exactly what I'm saying. How do you know she left of her own will? How do you know she wasn't snatched?"

Post hesitated. "The minute she saw the squad

car pull up in front of school, she ran. My police experience tells me that's not a kidnapping."

"What did you want to talk to her about?"

Post twisted his mouth, and when he didn't answer, I said, "Is this about that dead policeman?"

"What do you know about that?"

Blackie and I exchanged looks, with Post watching us like we were serial killers about to confess. "I'd tell you, Post, but you don't want hear it."

"Try me."

"Marina's I.D. is good. She's telling you the truth. That dead policeman killed our guy."

I'd hoped to see some sign in Post's face that he agreed, but all he did was study me for a few seconds like he was trying to figure out if I was lying or not. Then he said, "You got proof?"

"An eyewitness ought to count for something, don't you think?"

He snickered. "She turns up, you call me. Understand?"

"Fuck that," Blackie said as Post sauntered back to his car. But I was already inside, racing up the stairs, taking the steps two at a time.

The lock on the door didn't look jimmied and the door was intact. Marina didn't know enough to do a break-in without leaving some major clues along the way, but I called her name out anyway as I stepped into the darkened apartment.

I switched on the light and heard Blackie come in behind me. He held an unlit cigarette in one hand and a match in the other as he glanced around the empty room.

"Shoulda coached the kid on locks," he said, striking the match. Then he headed for the refrigerator. "Got any beer?"

I set the Cheerios box on the table and reached for the phone. Marina's aunt picked up on the third ring.

"What do they think she's done?" I asked once she'd told me that Post had been by.

Mrs. Murieta's voice trembled. "A *policia*," she said.

"Yes, that's right," I agreed, wondering why I was having trouble getting through to her now and hadn't in the past. "Philly Post. The lieutenant. He came by. I understand that."

"No," she answered. "*Otro policia*. Another *policia*, he is dead and the Lieutenant, he thinks *mi* Marina can tell him who committed this crime."

"Is that what he said?"

"No. Javier de Vega told me. He is Marina's friend. From school. The *policia*, they talked to Javier and then Javier called me. But I know nothing."

"When was the last time you saw Marina?"

"This morning. When you came to pick her up this morning."

Great. At least that explained why Post was looking at me. "Did Javier see her at school? Did he talk to her?"

"*Sí.*"

"Give me his number."

Right away Javier knew who I was. He told me Marina had ducked out of fourth period when she saw the police car pull up in front of school. She hadn't done her homework anyway. Javier told me he was positive Marina was all right, but swore he didn't know where she was. Even over the phone the kid couldn't lie worth a damn.

"Tell her to call me," I said, hoping that he'd been more believable with the police than he'd been with me. "Tell her I want to talk to her."

I hung up, wrapped my fingers around the cold dark beer Blackie had set in front of me, and lifted it to my lips. I hadn't realized how thirsty I was. Blackie watched me drink, then listened when I told him about Marina.

He stifled a belch. "Kid's got a good instinct."

"Running just makes you look guilty." I'd learned that the hard way.

"What kinda fair shake's she gonna get off Post? He stiffed her on the I.D., didn't he? Fuck's used to thinkin' with a two-by-four 'stead of a brain."

"Maybe you're right, Blackie." Post hadn't believed anything Marina had given him so far. Why would he change now? He'd probably pack her off to protective custody or juvenile detention and forget about her.

Blackie stubbed out his smoke and grunted. "Damn straight I'm right. Kid's better off on the lam."

But if somebody was hiding something worth killing for, something two people had died over,

Marina was in danger. Blackie cleared his throat. I followed his eyes to Sam Ackerman's cereal box on the table.

"The kid'll show up, doll," he said. "She can hang tough."

"Maybe." I wanted to believe him.

"Whataya got in the box?"

I pushed Marina from my mind for the time being, cleared a spot on the table, set my beer down, and up-ended the box of Cheerios. The mail I'd crammed in fell out first and a bunch of stuff came out on top of it. The last thing out of the box slipped off the pile of papers and fell onto the tabletop with a *clink*.

Blackie and I both stared. It was a key.

"Housekey?" Blackie asked.

I picked it up and read the tiny print etched into its head. TORKLEY. The same brand of lock he had on his front door. "I'm afraid you're right, Blackie. It must be his spare."

I set the key aside and started on the rest of the stuff in front of me. The first thing I pulled out of the pile was Sam Ackerman's Social Security card. The first three digits told me he was from Nevada. The next document confirmed it. His birth certificate said he'd been born in Sparks and that his mother's name was Eveline and his father was a shopkeeper named Arthur.

"What else, doll?"

I riffled through the rest of the documents. "He's been married and divorced. Mary Ellen Smith from Toledo. He's got medical insurance and twenty-one thousand dollars in an IRA account. He owns fifteen hundred shares of MCI stock. There's six thousand four hundred seventy-five dollars and thirty-five cents in a pass-book account in his name at Cal Fed."

I crammed those things back into the box of Cheerios and set it aside, then reached for the mail and started sorting through it.

"*Columbia Journalism Review* and *Wired*," I said, tossing the magazines one at a time on the floor at the foot of my chair. "A bill from PG&E, one from the cable TV company, and—what's this?"

The last envelope was addressed by hand. I glanced at the return address and my heart quickened.

"Seems our guy's got a pen pal in San Quentin," I said. I was thinking of the kid Lucho Navarro had brought to me, the one with the brother fresh out of San Quentin, as I reached for the letter opener. But the name at the bottom of the letter asking Ackerman to come see him wasn't Valentín or El Gordo or even the Fat Man or Herbie Caballos. It was Julius Stendahl.

I looked across at Blackie and repeated the name out loud. "Sound familiar?"

Blackie swigged down the last of his beer and set the empty down on the floor next to the couch. "Never heard of the bum. What's he got to say?"

The note was handwritten, printed neatly in tiny, meticulously formed letters interspersed with oddly placed capitalizations. I read it aloud:

deaR samUel I am suR I caN tell you eVerythiNg you need to Know because we were soul-
MateS and SOulmAtes knoW, all You onLy need
AsK ask and anser tHe TRUTH will be told and
she shaRed EvErything with me I CaN tell YoU
whaT you want.   EverYthing and, All   Come
Wensday aT 11 o-cLock or else I wiLl haVe to
carRy thiS BUrden and I would like her to be
aLive agAin siGned juliUs stendHal.

"Whew!" I handed the note to Blackie.

He studied it and said, "Fucker's on drugs.
Else he oughta be."

I picked up the envelope. "It's postmarked
yesterday. That means it probably was delivered
today."

Blackie shook his head in disgust and tossed
the letter on top of the rest of the stuff on the
table. "You're not thinkin' a talkin' to this
bongo?"

"He's a lead to Sam Ackerman's story,
Blackie. This could be the reason he was killed."

Blackie squinted at me. "Bad call, doll."

"Bad call or not, he's all I've got."

27

The drive to San Quentin is nothing short of spectacular: Across the Golden Gate Bridge and east toward the Richmond–San Rafael Bridge until the turnoff, then a short, winding drive past squat little cottages to a parking lot with million-dollar views of San Francisco. I guess a con could do worse for a view.

Administration had explained that you can't see a prisoner unless he agrees first to see you. So I put in the paperwork and waited. Two days later, just after I'd heard from an otherwise dodgy and sullen Marina that she was all right, the day after I'd called Checker and told him his dead man was Sam Ackerman, and while I was out on my morning run, a message came in on my answering machine. It was Julius Stendahl himself, his high-pitched feminine-sounding voice formal and excited at the same time.

"See you this afternoon," he had said. "Two o'clock."

And now here I was downshifting the Toyota as I rolled up to the big walls, wondering what Sam Ackerman had intended to ask Julius Stendahl.

The routine was the same as before back when I'd been a parole officer—leaving my stuff in the locker at the front gate, checking my shoes for shanks, and passing through a metal detector and two picture I.D. checkpoints before reaching the actual building where visitors are allowed inside.

Most of the people swarming around the tables in the open visiting room were heart-breaks—parents and buddies and girlfriends. But the women with children were the ones that got to me: sad-eyed and resigned, mostly black or Latina, clutching babies and comforting the oddly silent older kids, who didn't quite know what was going on but had figured out enough to know things could have been better.

Then they brought out Julius Stendahl and I forgot about all the rest. He strode in with a hopeful expression on his oily, moon-shaped face. Behind Coke-bottle-lensed glasses, bugged-out, pale, bloodshot eyes searched the room, not even pausing as they swept over me. He went over the room a second time, then a third, and that's when I raised my hand.

His expression when he realized who I was was so filled with disappointment I thought he might just turn around and walk back to his cell. But he stared me up and down, then came over to the rough-edged Formica-topped table where I sat.

He towered over me, studying me openly. So I stood up and studied him back. He was big and pear-shaped, with a fleshy layer of padding under shiny, pink skin, and wispy, baby-fine barely-there hair that straggled down to his shoulders. He was the creep everybody makes fun of in high school, the guy who never fit in and never would, all grown up and gone weird. He lacked the pumped-up muscles most of the guys around us had, but he had something the other guys were missing—a malevolence, an air of sickness that sort of hung over him and made my skin crawl. It made me wonder what kind of awful stuff Sam Ackerman was on to.

"You don't look anything like her," he finally said, staring hard at me with bug eyes, not bothering to hide his disappointment.

"Like who?"

"Olivia."

"Olivia?" Our eyes locked and for a moment I didn't understand. Then the realization hit me like a fist to the chest. It knocked the wind out of me.

"Olivia?"

He saw my shock and it seemed to please him. The corners of his mouth turned up just slightly.

"Yes," he said. "Olivia."

I forgot all about Sam Ackerman and Herbie Caballos. It was my turn to stare. "My mother? Are you talking about my mother?"

All I could think of was this weirdo and my mom. I couldn't picture somebody like him knowing her. I couldn't even picture somebody like him taking out her garbage. Why would Sam Ackerman write about my mother? Why would he even think she'd be connected to this creep? There had to be some kind of mistake.

"Are you talking about my mother, Mr. Stendahl?"

He suddenly let out a relieved kind of a snort. "This is great," he whispered with satisfaction. Then he pulled out a chair and sat down. "This all right."

I sat down, too, and asked in as even a tone as I could muster, "Who are you?"

I didn't like him. I didn't like being in the same room with him, much less sitting across the table with just two feet of space between us. But the man had answers—maybe. I checked to make sure the prison guards were still in the corners. They were, but they seemed miles away.

Stendahl smiled. His teeth were tiny and pointed, like he'd filed them down to make them sharp.

"You have her spirit," he said, then leaned forward in his chair and sort of sniffed the air like he was trying to smell me. I had to force myself not to recoil.

"I can see her in you," he said happily. "I'm glad you came to visit me."

"I didn't come to visit, Mr. Stendahl. I came for information." About Sam Ackerman. But what I asked instead was, "How did you know my mother?"

He closed his eyes, linked his fingers behind his neck so that his elbows stuck out on either side, and smiled languidly, like he was remembering something really special.

"Mr. Stendahl?"

He opened his eyes, and his nasty gaze burned into me. He watched my face like a cobra.

"Oh, yes," he whispered, and his smile got broader. "I knew her all right. Your mother and I, Miss Ventana, were *very* close. You could even say we were soul mates."

Soul mates? I felt the heat rise to my face. No way would my mother be involved with a nutcase like him. "You're full of shit," I said.

He smiled again. "Why? Because she never mentioned me? Well, she wouldn't. It was our secret."

I just stared.

"We were in love," he explained.

"Right. Sure. Look, mister, you're crazy."

It was the wrong thing to say. The guy was nuts, and the best way to deal with a nut is to humor him. But Stendahl didn't seem upset. He looked amused.

"You don't believe me because she never mentioned me. But see, she wouldn't have. Think about it. She wouldn't have. Why would she tell a lousy kid?"

"You're crazy." I shoved my chair back and started to rise.

"Wait!"

I froze. Part of me, the part that hungered to learn more about them, held me there.

Stendahl's words were low and urgent. "You can't see because you don't want to believe it. But what we had was pure and good and wonderful. It was special. We—Olivia and me—Olivia wanted to be with me more than anything in the world. You look like him and you probably think if she didn't like him, then she didn't like you. But I can tell you things, things you don't know about her, things she told me in confidence because it was me she trusted and loved. It was me. She loved *me*."

Maybe it was the conviction in his voice, maybe it was the promise, however hollow and unlikely, of hearing about a mother I'd like to have known better, or maybe it was just curiosity about what made this man lie with such conviction, but I dropped back into the chair.

"She *married* my father," I said, then realized how stupid it sounded. "Forget it."

I didn't even believe the guy. Why sit here and talk to him like he was sane? But his creepy bloodshot eyes locked onto mine.

"Our paths—Olivia's and mine—didn't cross until after she'd made the mistake of marrying the wrong man."

Something rumbled at the pit of my stomach and I tasted bile in my mouth. "You don't know what you're talking about."

His oily face turned suddenly mournful. "You talk like it was ugly. It wasn't. She was in love with me. She was only staying with him until she could work things out."

"That's not true," I said, shaking my head. "You're making all this up."

"Olivia"—he said her name like he was talking about God—"Olivia was too honorable to leave, but she loved me to the very end. I was going to help her—to leave. We were planning. I was getting things ready so she could come to me. Then she was killed."

Killed? *Killed?* I'd never thought of my parents being *killed*. They had *died*. I stared across the room at the row of windows high on the wall. Beyond the bars the sky was a deep cobalt blue. They had died.

I brought my gaze back to Stendahl and found him studying me with an intensity that made me want to punch his face.

"Look, mister. Whatever your game is, I'm not playing. You're sick. You and I both know you never met my mother. All you've got is some crazy imagination. I don't know what your problem is, but I'm not going to help you along with it." I pushed my chair back again and started to rise.

"April twenty-fourth," he said quickly and I froze.

I hesitated. April twenty-fourth. The date of the accident.

"She was wearing a black satin dress," he continued rapidly. "Gold beads on the collar."

"Anybody who can read a paper can find out that much." I rose and looked around for my backpack, then remembered I'd left it in the locker at the gatehouse.

"She sewed the beads on herself," he said quickly before I could turn to go. "Around the collar. One by one."

The memory of my mother sitting by the living room lamp the night before she died, stitching the tiny beads onto her dress filled me with longing. And fear. How could he have known? I stared into his shining, putty-colored face. He smiled.

"I was there," Stendahl whispered.

Slowly I dropped back into the chair. "In my house?"

His narrow lips twisted with annoyance. "On April twenty-fourth," he repeated. "I was there. I saw Olivia die."

38

A hot pressure burned behind my eyes. Julius Stendahl was talking. His lips were moving, but I couldn't hear what he was saying. Then his voice broke through the roaring inside my head.

". . . know someone was following her?"

I blinked. "*You* followed them?"

He smiled, satisfied. He had me now and he knew it. My chest felt tight. I couldn't breathe.

"Did you see the accident, Mr. Stendahl? Are you saying you were there when they crashed?"

He nodded serenely.

"Is that why Sam Ackerman wanted to talk to you?"

"I can see her spirit in your eyes," he said softly, almost to himself. "She must have sent you to me."

"Tell me what you saw."

He set his hands on the table and pushed himself up, watching me, smiling that annoying satisfied smile. "I'll tell you next time. Come see me Thursday."

"No! Wait! Don't go." I grabbed his fleshy wrist. He was bigger than me by about a hundred pounds and a whole lot stronger, but he froze when I touched him. The guards started toward us, then retreated to their posts when I let go.

Julius Stendahl sat back down slowly, a look of enormous pleasure on his pale, round features.

That's when it hit me: He'd *wanted* me to touch him. I'd given him some sort of weird rush, and the thought left me feeling dirty. I pushed the cold revulsion aside and took a deep breath.

"What did you see, Mr. Stendahl?"

"Call me Julius. May I call you Veronica?"

"Just tell me what you saw."

"You called Olivia's death an accident. It wasn't an accident," he said lightly.

The roar in my head started up again. It was so loud and powerful, I had to struggle to understand. "You killed them?" I asked stupidly.

Stendahl looked appalled. "No! I'd never hurt Olivia. I'd die for her myself. It was somebody else."

"If you know something, just say it."

"If you don't believe me, ask Sam Ackerman. He'll back me up. I bet by now he even knows who killed her."

A huge rush of sound filled my head again. "What? What are you saying?"

Julius Stendahl smiled patiently, like he was talking to a dear, loved child. "Sam Ackerman knows. That's why he wrote to me. Someone was following her. Somebody besides me. Your parents didn't run up on that median by themselves, Veronica. Somebody made them do it. And somebody forced them into that light pole. I know because I *saw* it happen. *I was there.*"

39

I sat in my car out in the San Quentin parking lot and stared across the water to the City. The sun was out and the sky was so blue and so clear it made your eyes ache to look at it. The day after my parents died had been like this—bright and crisp and sunny. The brightness all around me that day twenty years ago made the hurt seem sharper. I had wanted fog, gray, soothing fog and lonely foghorns moaning in the distance. I'd wanted the world, or at least the city, to mourn with me.

I sat here now and remembered the odd little things I'd remembered that day and the long days after they died. I remembered the way my dad would gracefully fold back his starched, white cuffs before he'd work a practice lock, how they'd each watch the other move across a room with a mixture of admiration and pride. I remembered my mother pulling things off her dresser, then mine, and stuffing everything into a suitcase for a surprise trip to Mendocino or Carmel or Big Sur. I remembered the warmth I'd felt watching them dance at Frankie Zola's wedding and thinking they looked more beautiful and more in love than Frankie and his bride. The soft touch of my mother's hand on my fevered cheek when I was ill and my father's reassuring embrace, so full of love and warmth that whenever he hugged me, I'd always prayed that he'd never let go.

And then I remembered the phone calls, the times I'd answer and no one would speak, the times my father would shout angrily into the phone. I remembered my mother saying, "Don't bother, 'Cisco. It's just a crush. The boy is harmless." And the doorbell ringing and more shouts and my mother refusing to go anywhere by herself. That haunted look I thought she got because of the trial.

I sat in my car in the parking lot of San Quentin and realized that the carefully constructed assumptions I'd made when I was fourteen didn't add up. I'd blamed the reporters for my parents' turmoil. But the reporters had all loved my parents. They respected them and partied with them. My father wouldn't have shouted at them. My mother wouldn't have hid from them.

I gazed at the big concrete mass that was San Quentin and realized Julius Stendahl had been at the root of the fear and anger that had darkened my parents' last days. And I wondered if Julius Stendahl was going to answer old questions or just open old wounds.

40

The young, muscled-up guy standing on the sidewalk in front of my building was either a bouncer or a boxer. He looked more brave than bright, and in spite of his size, he gave the impression of being light on his feet.

He watched me approach and waited until I had my key in the door before he spoke.

"You Ventana?"

I met his gaze and tried to look as tough as he did. "Who wants to know?"

He blinked, hesitated, then offered me his surprisingly small hand. "Kid Glove Garuch," he said, with a dignified nod. "I understand you talked to that scum-sucker Stendahl."

"What makes you think that?"

"I got friends."

I waited, not saying yes or no.

"He's scum," Garuch said. "He's a stalker. You talk to him, could be he starts stalkin' you next."

"So what if he does? What do you care?"

"Maybe I don't. But I want him to do hard time. Visits break up the routine, make the time go faster."

I pushed the door open. "Thanks for sharing, Mr.—Garuch, is it? I make it a point not to get involved in other people's business. You ought to try it. Saves a lot of trouble all the way around."

I started to step inside, but he grabbed my arm, gently, like he was acutely aware of his strength, and said, "Wait!"

I stopped, and stared at his hand until he let go.

"Please," he said, then glanced away. When he brought his blue eyes back to meet mine, pain had softened the anger I'd seen there before.

"That bastard kidnapped my wife," he said evenly. "He stalked her and he tormented her and then he kidnapped her. And all he's doin' to pay for it is three years. Three lousy years. That ain't even close to enough for what he did to her."

I vaguely remembered reading about a man being sentenced to prison around a year ago for stalking a ballerina. I'd noticed the article because the picture the paper ran with the story showed a woman who could have been my mother's twin.

"Is your wife—?"

"—Minette Ogilvie."

So that meant he was a boxer. Blackie knew him. He'd talked about how Garuch was in jail for roughing up the stalker when the stalker kidnapped Minette.

"When I got together with Minette, this loser'd

been crowding her for ten years. He picked her out of a group shot they ran in the *Chronicle* when Minette was thirteen. An' back then this guy's what, maybe thirty years old? He's sick. What's a guy thirty years old want with a kid, you know?

"Letters an' calls, an' every performance she's ever done, he's there. Ten years she's been telling this limp dick to get lost and he can't get the message. He'd show up every place she went."

"He followed her?"

"Yeah."

Kid kept talking, but all I heard was my mother's long-silent voice from an overheard conversation twenty years ago.

"Oh, 'Cisco, he's only a boy. You saw him. It's a mere infatuation. That's why he follows me," I remembered her saying. *"Next week it'll be his math teacher."*

"It's been longer than a week, querida. And the letters. I will take care of him."

"No, 'Cisco. He's harmless. The letters are all professions of love. He wouldn't harm someone he loves. Really. You mustn't. Especially now with the trial. Please, darling, don't jeopardize the trial."

I looked up. Garuch was still talking, his face sour with the memory.

"I thought it was some kinda joke the first time she told me about him. Then I saw what she was up against. I told the guy to back off. I told him to get lost. I told him his future depended on him bowing out. Nothin'. This guy keeps comin' back for more."

Garuch shrugged. "So I worked him over.

Let's say I delivered the message. That got me two months in jail. Go figure—he's harassin' *us* and *I* end up in jail. When I was gone, that's when the creep makes his move."

He shut his jaw, and the muscles in his neck stood out like thick steel cables. His fists were clenched. "He told Minette they were getting married. Showed her a wedding dress he bought for her. The piece of shit knew she was already married to me, but he just acted like I didn't exist.

"I woulda killed him if I hadn't been locked up. I swear I woulda. By the time I got out, he was locked up and Minette got the first peace she's had in eleven years. That's the only thing that's saved his ass so far, him being locked up."

Kid pointed a finger at me. "You find out this guy's on the streets again, you tell me. He won't give nobody no grief when I'm done with him."

"Did he ever try to physically harm Minette?" If he had tried to hurt her, he might have hurt my mom. He could have caused the accident.

But Kid Glove shook his head. "Never laid a finger on her, but that don't mean he didn't hurt her. Man, she came this close"—he raised a thick thumb and index finger and held them about an eighth of an inch apart—"this close to just plain losing it. She can't handle too much of anything anymore. She cut back on the performances, an' we take a lot of vacations 'cause she just can't handle any kind of pressure anymore. An' friends? Forget it! She don't trust nobody unless they're related or they went to first grade with her. Or if they're with me, then they're okay. She don't even trust the law that much after what they pulled on us there at the end."

"You mean arresting you instead of Stendahl?" I asked.

"Huh-uh. After he snatched her. D.A.'s workin's with us, tellin' us how he's gonna go for the full eight years—the max on kidnapping. Then what happens? Coupla cops show up and say the creep's all right. They ask the judge ta go light, and the judge, he does it! He buys these lousy cops' stories."

"What did they say?"

"The younger guy—well, he was in his forties, but the other guy looked older—so he gets up there and starts in on how the creep put his life on the line, testifying against some skell dealing drugs. Then he goes on to say the guy had a clean record, so they oughta give him the three years instead of the eight. So bing bang, just like that, the judge goes for the three! I couldn't believe it. I says to the D.A., 'Aren't you an' the cops supposed to be on the same side?' and he just, you know, gives me the big shine on, shrugs, an' says he did the best he could."

"What do you want from me, Mr. Garuch?"

"Leave him alone. Freeze 'im out. Make him do the hard time."

The last thing I could picture myself doing was going back to see Julius Stendahl.

I pushed the door open again and said, "I'll give it every consideration, Mr. Garuch. Good-bye."

41

started where I thought Sam Ackerman might have started. Before Herbie Caballos and the Fat Man, before Harland Harper and before Julius Stendahl. I went back twenty years.

I hadn't been able to bear reading the stuff about the trial when it was going on, much less the huge write-ups after the accident, but I spent the next three hours at the newspaper morgue immersed in the public version of my parents' lives:

. . . the sophisticated couple waved confidently at the huge crowd of supporters as they entered City Hall, where they would stand trial for burglary; blue-blooded Olivia Sutton Ventana, the toast of the San Francisco Debutante Ball twenty years ago, stood strong and brave amid the indictments against her and her rakish husband. . . .

They described the clothes my mother wore and marveled at the cut of my father's suits. They even tagged my handsome father a "strong-featured, swarthy Adonis" and a "renegade rogue," which made me laugh, even if in my four-teen-year-old-child's memory he was the most beautiful man I'd ever seen.

After reading all that stuff I felt a different kind of sadness. My heart was heavy, not with the usual realization they'd been taken from me but with the devastating knowledge that maybe I'd never really known them at all. I'd seen one facet, maybe two, but they'd both been so rare and so complex, so richly unique. And I'd lost them so young. I would never know them fully no matter what I did or what happened.

Beyond making me depressed, the stuff in the paper was close to useless. I'd read it all and I didn't know any more than I had before. Everything was surface—no substance. I guess I shouldn't have been surprised. But where did Sam Ackerman get his tip? Had he seen something I'd missed? I started all over again and reread everything, but nothing turned up.

I was scuttling all the clips back into the moldy envelope I'd found them in when the door opened and a hunched-over old man shuffled into the room. His clothes—a red cardigan sweater and loose-fitting pants that bagged out at the knees—looked moth-eaten and dusty. He had dim blue eyes behind a scholarly set of bifocals and skin that looked like buffalo hide.

"Excuse me," he said softly. "You're Miss Ventana."

It wasn't a question, so I didn't answer.

He muttered something to himself, then rubbed the back of one gnarled hand against the palm of the other as the door closed behind him with a gentle *swish*.

"I'm Reece Cunningham," he said. "I—"

I glanced down at the byline on the clippings in my hand. "You covered the trial."

His nod was stately. "The librarian told me you were here. I came down because I wanted to meet you."

I set the clippings on the table and we shook hands. His was cold and rough and bony. "Sit down, Ms. Ventana, please."

He shuffled over to one of the chairs and made a soft grunt as he dropped into it. His breathing was raspy and rough, like taking those couple of steps had worn him out.

"Too many smoke-filled deadlines," he explained. There was something faintly of the South in his voice. "I'm an editor here now. But not for long. I'm retiring in a few weeks." He nodded to himself, like he was trying to get used to the idea.

I glanced at the folder full of clippings and when I looked up, his eyes were alert and trained on me.

"I suppose everyone comments on the resemblance," he said. "It's uncanny. You are a female replica of 'Cisco himself."

"Mr. Cunningham, has anybody asked you about my parents? I mean lately?"

His old eyes studied me shrewdly for a

moment. "You must have run into Sam Ack-erman before he died."

"He talked to you?"

The old man nodded. "Damn shame about him. Made copies of all of that," he said, gesturing toward the envelope in my hand.

"Did he say why?"

"Didn't say he was copying it. Caught him by accident down at the copy machine, tried to hide what he was doing. I wouldn't have noticed the clips 'cept the day before, he showed up down at the bar where I always take my lunch. Sits down and starts talking Giants, the next thing I know, smooth as a snake, he's turned the whole thing into what amounted to an interview about the Ventana cat burglars. He's so good at it I didn't even catch on until I thought about it later that night. You know how he did it so smooth? He starts out asking me questions, real vague, sort of casual questions, and all of a sudden I bring up 'Cisco and Olivia Ventana, like it's my idea to talk about them. He didn't even act interested. He tried to change the subject the first time. Least that's how it felt. Boy was good. Deserved every bit of that Pulitzer he got."

The old man added, "Police are calling his death a routine mugging. What do you think?"

"I don't know what to think, Mr. Cun-ningham. Do you have any ideas?"

"Not anymore. I'm too old for ideas. I'm retiring. I'll leave it to youngsters like you."

"What did Sam Ackerman want to know?"

"Got me. That boy plays it close to the vest. Did he come and talk to you?"

"Not exactly. But I think whoever killed him thinks he did."

That would fit in with the message theory. The killer might have thought I'd sicced Ackerman onto the story and by killing him and dumping him under my nose, I'd get the warning to back off.

"Did you know my parents, Mr. Cunningham?"

"Oh, yes, of course." He smiled warmly. "Wonderful people! Larger than life—a reporter's dream. Olivia—uh, your mother, I mean—didn't ever say much, but then, she didn't need to. One smile and a kind word and she had the world eating out of her hand. I believe she knew her power, but she never let on. The gracious ones never do. She had grace and class, you know? She was a lady.

"And 'Cisco was the same but different. His charm was all in talking to you. He'd fix on you like you're the only fella he's gonna tell this story to. Ninety-nine percent of what he told me was off the record, but the one percent that went into print was still enough to seal the legend." He chuckled. "Big hearts," he said. "Big, big hearts and enough style and panache to make stealing jewels off the rich folks look like they were doing everybody a favor. No, this city'll never see the likes of their kind of style again."

His eyes wandered to the clipping on the table. "I was very sorry when they died, Ms. Ventana. And not just because they made great copy, either." He smiled wistfully. "I'd been day-dreaming about a Pulitzer for covering that trial, but never mind that. We lost a real piece of San Francisco when they passed on." He gestured to the folder. "I tried to make sure as many people as possible realized that."

"Is that what you told Sam Ackerman?"

He nodded. "More or less. We talked about their personalities of course."

"Did you tell him about Julius Stendahl?"

"That crazy kid? He was driving them both nuts. Sendin' Olivia all those love letters and makin' a nuisance of himself. Only reason 'Cisco didn't have some of his buddies take care of the kid was Olivia felt sorry for him. She was scared, but not scared enough to let 'Cisco take action."

"Did you talk to Stendahl yourself?"

He shook his head. "Olivia told me about him."

"What else did Ackerman ask about?"

"Well, naturally I told him about the night they died. He acted like he didn't know anything about it. He grew up in Nevada, you know, so he wasn't around San Francisco twenty years ago."

"Tell me what you told him. Did you go out there that night, Mr. Cunningham? The night of the accident? Were you there?"

His eyes narrowed. He answered carefully. "Ye-e-ss."

"Did you take any notes?"

"I don't need notes to remember that night."

"The accident happened at two o'clock. What time did you get there?"

He shifted in his chair and looked uncomfortable, but his tired old eyes seemed kind. "Why are you here, Miss Ventana?"

I hesitated. "There's a chance, Mr. Cunningham, that there was a second car involved in the accident that killed my parents."

He blinked. "Who told you that? Did Sam tell you that?"

"I never spoke to Sam."

"Then who?"

"A possible witness." I still wasn't sure if Stendahl was jamming me around on that point and whether he'd been doing the same with Ackerman.

"A witness? To the accident?" Cunningham shook his wrinkled head. "There were no witnesses, Miss Ventana."

"You sound pretty sure of that."

"I am." He ran his tongue over cracked, dry lips. "The police looked things over. The insurance people looked things over. *I* looked things over. If there was evidence that another car was involved, don't you think someone might have come forward?"

His expression softened. "Forgive me for saying this, Miss Ventana, but your parents are dead. They've been dead for almost twenty years now, and nothing you do is ever going to change that fact."

"I'm not trying to change the facts, Mr. Cunningham, I'm trying to *find* them. Sam Ackerman seemed to think something was off. Didn't you see anything that could mean there was another car there that night?"

He sighed. "What would you gain if you could prove a second car was involved?"

"I'm not sure. I guess I just need to know."

He studied me for what seemed like a full minute, then seemed to come to some sort of decision. "All right, then," he said. "Come on. I'll show you something."

With a lot of effort and a lot of wheezing, he pushed himself out of his chair and trudged to the door. He paused there and beckoned to me.

I followed him down the hall to an elevator, then rode up two floors and made my way behind him through a rat's maze of desks and cubicles to a small room with a small window looking out onto Mission Street.

Cunningham rummaged through a black file cabinet, then spread three faded eight-by-ten black-and-white photographs on the desk top beside the file cabinet.

"There," he said. "See for yourself."

I hung back, suddenly unsure. "Are they . . . ?"

"The accident," he answered, nodding and shuffling the sheets around on his desk, I guess so I could get a better look. When I didn't step up beside him, he turned, a puzzled expression on his face. Then his eyes softened.

"Oh," he said, and started gathering up the pictures. "Tell you what, Miss Ventana. I don't need these old pictures for anything right now. I'm retirin' in a couple of weeks anyway and nobody's going to miss them. Why don't you just take them? How does that sound?"

He was standing in front of me, envelope extended, a sincerely apologetic expression on his old face.

"When you do look—" he began, but I interrupted him, muttering something about another appointment and starting for the door.

He shoved the envelope with surprising force and speed into my hands and called out after me as I hurried out of his office.

"You'll see. When you look. There's just one set of skid marks. One car. Whoever told you there was another car, Miss Ventana, is playing a cruel, cruel hoax."

42

I drove around with that envelope on the floor of the passenger side of my car until dusk. Then I carried it into the Quarter Moon with me and stared at it through three beers, then four.

When I finally opened it, I was upstairs in my apartment, alone.

Cold fingers clutched my heart and froze me from the inside out as I spread them one by one on the table I use for a desk. Of all the times I'd imagined how it must have been, I never once had come even close to the stark brutality I saw now.

The first photograph was dark and sort of fuzzy. The scene in the center was lighted, but all around the edges of the frame the world was black.

I blinked and forced myself to focus on the picture, on the photograph, on the stark shapes frozen in time. The mangled BMW roadster—my parents' car—rested, smashed to bits against the unyielding post. The front hood was accordioned to a third of the size it had been, and the gleaming silver paint was charred black.

Tiny, white specks littered the pavement around the car. Glass—broken bits of glass from the windshield and the headlights and the windows had caught the light from the camera's flash and lay sprinkled like diamonds all around the battered car.

"My God." I felt like a big hole had opened up inside me and I was fourteen all over again, raw with pain and freshly abandoned. I wanted to turn away, run out of the room and out of the building. I wanted to keep running until I could forget. But I knew I couldn't.

The second photograph wasn't any easier to look at. The front end of an ambulance showed in the lower right-hand corner. It was still night.

I blinked to steady myself against the hurt and looked closer. The photographer had moved to the other side of the car, the driver's side, and I could see that the damage was worse there. *My God.*

I made myself look at the third picture just so I would stop staring at that driver's-side door. The photographer had backed up some distance and taken a long shot that included the skid marks on the pavement. The photo showed that my father had slammed on the brakes about fifteen feet from the median, then at the last minute twisted the car so that his side took the brunt of the impact.

There weren't any other tire marks in the picture. I stared at the picture, letting the horror and grief wash through me, then letting it seep slowly out of my bones.

Finally, when I felt numb enough and strong enough, I picked up the pictures and put them back in the envelope. I put the envelope in a box at the back of my closet and sat quietly on the roof, sipping beer, watching the city lights twinkle, and going over every single memory of my parents' brief life, one by one, until the sun came up.

43

I guess the reason I left the whole thing alone for the next couple of days was because of the bruises chalked up from looking at those pictures. The car had looked so frail and mangled. And I kept thinking about my parents being inside it when it crashed. No matter what I did, I couldn't get that image out of my mind.

A man had come to talk to me the day after the accident to tell me that they hadn't suffered, that they'd died instantly, but I still had to wonder what had gone through their hearts those last few seconds. Had they known they were going to die? Were they afraid?

Those pictures had stirred up deep feelings I'd buried, feelings I thought I'd gotten past. But now the wounds were raw all over again, and fresh.

Then on Thursday, right after I'd got in from a long, soothing run out to Fort Point and back, right after I'd finally convinced myself that it was the S.F.P.D.'s job to figure out who killed Sam

Ackerman and why, right after I'd decided just to leave the whole thing alone, the phone rang.

"Ronnie?"

The voice, a man's voice, was hoarse and intimate. It raised the hairs at the back of my neck.

"Who is this?" I asked.

"It's Julius, Ronnie. Remember me?"

All the pain and all the sadness from the last couple of weeks burned away into one hard ball of anger.

"I remember you all right. You're the crank trying to jerk me around. Well, hear this," I said. My throat constricted and my voice started to rise. "Your little scheme isn't working, mister. Take your pathetic little life and your stupid old stories and go to hell. Don't ever call me again!"

I slammed the receiver down and paced the small space of the room. My hands were shaking. My breath was coming in short little gasps and my heart was racing. I was halfway to the fridge for a beer before I stopped. I didn't need a drink. It was ten o'clock in the morning.

I went back to the table and sat down. I shouldn't have reacted like that. Stendahl had wanted to push my buttons and I had let him. I took a deep breath. Next time he called, I'd be calm. I'd be cold and clinical. I wouldn't let him rattle me.

Then the phone rang again.

I let it ring once. Then twice. By the third ring I was calm. I'd convinced myself he wouldn't call back so soon. I picked up the receiver.

"Did you check things out?"

It was Stendahl. I took a second deep breath

to steady my voice and willed my heart to stop pounding. When I spoke, my words came out measured and even.

"There was no other car, Mr. Stendahl. Your tip was bad."

"You have to dig harder. They don't want you to know the truth."

Before I could catch myself, I said, "Who's 'they'?"

"*They.* The ones who killed Olivia."

I clutched the phone receiver to my ear and closed my eyes. Reece Cunningham was right. There were no witnesses. There was no second car. Stendahl didn't know. He hadn't been there that night. He hadn't seen a thing. He was making it all up.

"Look, Mr. Stendahl. I'm going to hang up now and you're not going to call me anymore, understand? If you call me again, ever, just once, I'll make sure the next time your warden lets you get close to a phone, you'll have forgotten how to use one."

He didn't call back and I thought that was it— until I went through my mail on Saturday. The note came in a plain white envelope addressed in perfect, tiny handprinted letters, some capitalized, some not. The short message inside—just one sentence on the single unlined sheet of cheap white paper—was in the same tiny print. It said simply,

why weRe they drIving nOrTH

He hadn't bothered to sign it, but I knew who'd sent it.

44

The pink flesh on Julius Stendahl's bare arms and neck jiggled as he crossed the room toward me. His round face and the thin, wispy hair that surrounded it were slick and oily—as dirty and soiled as I felt just being back here in his presence. But he was smiling, smiling and looking pleased with himself.

When he reached the table, as soon as he sat down, I said, "Where did they go?"

His smile lost a touch of its luster. The bulging eyes seemed to narrow a little, like he was trying to protect himself from a harsh wind. "Aren't you going to say hello?"

"I want to know where they went, Mr. Stendahl."

"Please, call me Julius."

"Fine. Julius. Where did they go?"

He smiled. "That's better. I like the way you say my name. It's nice. Olivia said it like that too. The same way."

He paused, and I was about to ask him again, when he said, "I was wondering if you could do me a favor."

"I'm not here to do favors."

"Do you have any pictures, any private pictures of Olivia? I know you probably treasure them, but mine, well, mine are starting to fade. And I was thinking—"

"Mr. Stendahl. Julius. I'm not going to play this little game with you. I need information and I need it now. Where did my parents go after they left the party?"

I'd spent the morning calling the surviving handful of people who I knew had been at the party twenty years ago, but after the first three I'd stopped. The inevitable pity in their voices was too much. Besides, they all said my parents hadn't told them a thing. Everybody assumed they were going home.

"Will you bring me a picture of Olivia if I tell you?"

"No." It didn't matter if I never found out where they'd gone that night; I was not going to help this weirdo get off on my mom.

"You disappoint me." Stendahl planted his hands on the table and started to heft himself up out of his chair.

"Anything else," I said quickly. "Ask for anything but that."

He kept his hands on the table and sank his soft bulk back down into the chair again. "Then I want a picture of you," he said.

"Don't do this, Mr. Stendahl."

"You said 'anything.' I like to have pictures of my friends."

"I'm not your friend."

"You should be, Veronica. I can help you. I can help you bury those demon memories."

"How? You're not giving me anything."

"Tit for tat, my dear Veronica. Nothing in this life is free. I'm paying now for a few lovely moments I had alone with a former love. The price was high, but I was willing to pay it. If you want to know what I know, the price isn't cheap. I want justice, too, but I'm not going to give it away."

I stared at his pink, oily skin, quivering from the effort of his labored breathing. I couldn't tell if he was having trouble taking in air because he was excited or just because he was overweight. His bloodshot eyes watched me.

"Tell me what you know," I repeated.

"Your photograph?"

"I'm not going to give you a picture, Julius. You might as well deal with that right now."

He looked chastened. "Will you at least come visit me?"

When I didn't answer, he said, "You're just like her, you know. She was strong and sharp, like that. I just wish you looked more like her. But you're exactly like her in everything else. Do you know that?"

I kept staring at him without answering. After a moment he gave in. "They left the party and drove through the park to Sunset Boulevard."

"And?"

"And I followed them. Unless you bring me your picture and a picture of Olivia, you'll never know where I followed them to."

I stood up and looked down into his shiny, big-pored face. "Fine," I said. "If that's how you want to play it, Stendahl, go ahead. Take it to your stinking grave."

45

Philly Post looked up from reading the note I'd tossed onto his cluttered desk and stared at me. I'd expected a scowl from him and he wasn't scowling. His expression was calm beneath thundercloud brows that hid most of his eyes.

"Am I supposed to know what this is about?" he asked.

"It's a lead on something I'm working. Not the cop killing," I said quickly. "It's something else. It's—well, actually, I'm looking into my parents' death."

"Turn over the kid and we'll talk."

I hadn't heard from Marina or Javier in days, and I'd been too caught up in my own drama to look for her. "I don't know where Marina is, Post, so drop it. Listen, there's this guy, Stendahl. Julius Stendahl. He's kind of a sicko, but he tipped me to the fact there was a second car involved."

Now he scowled.

"You talking about that loser that snatched the ballerina?"

I gave him an abbreviated version, leaving out everything connecting Stendahl to Ackerman and the dead undercover policeman, especially the part about breaking into Ackerman's house and stealing his mail.

When I finished, Post's face closed up. All of a sudden he started sending out signals that he didn't want to talk to me anymore. He glanced down at Stendahl's note—the one I'd tossed onto his desk—and shoved the note back toward me. He picked up a folder from his In-box, set it aside, then picked up another and started to examine it.

"I'm not going to go away, Post. I'm not leaving until you talk to me about this."

Philly Post sighed. He slapped shut the folder in front of him and looked at me from across the desk.

"Christ," he said with a second, even more dramatic sigh.

He didn't sound angry or annoyed, he just sounded surprised. "I can't believe you're letting some lunatic jerk you over like this. Don't give him the power. That's how these nuts operate. They dangle some kind of hope in front of you and then you're hooked. Don't let him jam you up like this, Ventana. He doesn't know shit."

"How do you know? Have you talked to him?"

"I don't need to talk to him. We get calls and nut mail from kooks like this all the time."

"I don't think he's so crazy."

What little sympathy there'd been in Post's expression vanished. "You a shrink now too?"

"If he can't think straight, then why did he bring this up? The fact that they were going north toward Marcel's house is relevant, Post. It's significant."

He rolled his eyes. "Yeah, right. I've seen these guys operate, Ventana. They're nothing but get-a-life geeks. All he's doing is stringing you out. There's nothing to what he's saying. The sooner you realize that, the better off you'll be."

"I want to see the accident report."

Post stared like he thought he hadn't heard me right. Then he rearranged himself in his chair and let out a long, husky sigh. "Forget it, Ventana."

"Post, look, it's—" Important? He knew that. My throat seemed to close up and a sudden tightness gripped my chest. I took a deep breath and looked at him. "Please," I said.

"Why? What's it going to get you?"

I reached into the backpack on the floor at my feet and pulled out a weathered blue receipt. The paper was soft and the faded ink of the handwriting that covered the back had seeped into the fibers so that the edges of the letters looked fuzzy. I set it down on Post's cluttered desk, writing side down, and pointed at the preprinted form on the front.

"My mother had the oil in the car changed that day. This is the receipt from the garage. She wrote me a note on the back telling me they were going to Marcel and Henri's for a party." I'd kept the note in my wallet for a year, then after that next to my birth certificate and my passport in my top dresser drawer.

Post glanced at the receipt and waited.

"Here." I tapped the faded, inked-in numbers in the upper right-hand corner of the page. "This is the odometer reading. See? Thirty-one thousand and thirty-six miles."

Post blinked.

"I drove the distances myself this morning after I talked to Stendahl," I said. "I drove from where Kurt's garage used to be on Columbus, to my parents' old house six blocks away, then to Marcel and Henri's. It's exactly six miles."

"Yeah? So?"

"Marcel and Henri live out on Fulton."

Post shifted in his chair and, in spite of himself, sort of nodded. He said, "And since Fulton is north of Golden Gate Park, that means your folks didn't have any business being on Sunset, which is south of the park, at two in the morning if they were on their way home from their friends' house. Is that the point you're making?"

"Right!" I slid back in my chair triumphantly. "*That's* why I need to see the report."

"I told you, it's not going to get you anything."

Maybe he didn't understand. Carefully, in as even a tone as I could muster, I explained. "I check the odometer reading on the accident report. I compare it to what I've got. That gives me an idea of how far they went."

"Still doesn't get you squat, Ventana. So they

took a drive around Lake Merced before heading home."

For one crazy minute I considered telling him that Sam Ackerman had been investigating my parents' death when Herbie Caballos and the Fat Man had killed him. But then he'd go orbital and shove me out of his way while his precious Tweedledum and 'Dee bungled their way through. I was positive Checker hadn't told Post I'd been the one to I.D. the Doe.

All I wanted was the mileage my parents had traveled. "Can I just see the report, Post?"

He looked at me funny, then reached for the In-box. For a split second I thought he'd been holding the file there all along and was going to give it to me. But it must have been just one more homicide file he needed to review, because he opened it and started reading, then looked across his desk at me.

"Walk, Ventana," he said. "We're done."

46

aybe Philly Post was done, but I wasn't. I rode the elevator up one floor to Aldo Stivick's office. Aldo might only be in Administration, but he's got access to practically everything. And sometimes, if I let him buy me lunch, he tells me stuff the rest of the police department considers privileged.

He was poring over a computer printout when I stepped into his office.

"So, Aldo," I said, and maybe I was a little too transparently enthusiastic, because when he looked up and saw me, his bland features registered caution instead of the usual puppy-dog eagerness he generally exhibited when he saw me.

"Ronnie," he said warily.

"It's been a while, hasn't it?"

"Uh—we talked last week. Remember?"

I guess I was obvious about not remembering because he added, "I asked you to go to the Ice Capades with me last Thursday."

And I'd said no. He couldn't hold that against me—I'd never gone out with him on a *date* date. I smiled, glanced casually down at the papers on his desk, and tried to stifle the guilt for what I was about to do. "Are you busy? I was thinking, it's almost noon, Aldo. Lunchtime. Are you free?"

His sudden over-eager smile made my stomach twist with guilt. Even in the service of justice I still feel bad about capitalizing on Aldo's feelings for me and his relentless capacity for trust. Anybody else would have called him a patsy, but to me Aldo was a good, reliable source.

He folded up his printout and was out the door and into the elevator before I could even think about changing my mind.

"How about Sammy's?" I asked as we stepped out into the sunlight on Bryant Street.

Sammy's is a combination falafel and Chinese joint down the block off Bryant. The place caters to lawyers and cops, two species of workers who, when they're around the Hall of Justice, are usually in a hurry. That was the plan: Lunch could be had at Sammy's in record time.

Aldo's face fell. "Oh," he said.

I made a big show of looking at my watch and seeming regretful. "I'm sort of in a rush, Aldo. I've got to be in the East Bay by two o'clock," I lied.

He made pouting noises and intimated canceling, and I considered just telling him up front that all I wanted was to see the damn file on my parents' accident, but with Aldo a little buttering up goes a long way. I made soothing remarks that didn't actually promise but implied that we'd do lunch again some other time. Soon.

And it worked. Seven minutes after leaving the Hall of Justice we were seated in a booth at Sammy's, hot falafels on our plates. Aldo was working his sandwich with all the gusto of a finicky Pekingese, I guess maybe because the falafel tasted like Sammy should have changed the grease in his frying vat a couple of dozen falafels ago. I couldn't complain. As far as I was concerned, I'd eat just about anything as long as I didn't have to fix it myself.

I made small talk until we were halfway through the meal, then I told Aldo that I'd come across information that maybe my parents' death wasn't an accident.

"That's horrible, Ronnie. Gosh, what if it wasn't? Who—?"

"If it wasn't, I'm going to find the killer."

"Wuh—wuh, yeah! But the police should investigate, too, Ronnie."

I nibbled lettuce from my sandwich while Aldo explained that there's no statute of limitations on homicide and that the police would surely investigate.

"That's just it, Aldo. My source isn't a hundred percent reliable. I need to make sure the information's solid before I bring the police into it."

"Oh, right. Of course," he agreed, nodding. "Yeah. Homicide's really backed up these days."

Aldo took a reluctant bite of falafel, chewed thirty times, then swallowed gingerly and asked, "Where would you start?"

I smiled. Aldo's so *easy*. I felt a twinge of guilt, but it passed quickly. After all, he'd given me my cue.

"I should probably take a look at the accident file. Do the police keep records that far back?"

Something like comprehension flickered across Aldo's face, but I guess he was just thinking, because all he said was, "I doubt it, but I can see. I can get you a copy if we do."

"Oh, Aldo!" I said. "You're terrific!"

He basked in the compliment, not exactly chattering away, because staid people like Aldo never chatter, but coming close. Then he sobered and glanced across the table at me.

"That would be really awful, Ronnie, if it's true that somebody killed your folks. I think you need to get to the bottom of this right away. So you can put it to rest."

I was touched at first, then I realized what he meant. Between the lines he was saying he doubted there'd been foul play and he wanted me to eliminate the possibility from my mind.

"It was a fairly reliable source," I said, contradicting myself without thinking.

"I'm sorry to hear that, Ronnie."

Aldo's expression was unmistakable: pity. I shoved my plate away. "How soon can you see about that file?"

He glanced at the plastic digital watch strapped precisely to his left wrist. "Want me to look for it now?"

47

I spent a couple of minutes mumbling into the pay phone outside the rest rooms at Sammy's pretending to cancel my fictitious East Bay appointment while the dial tone hummed in my ear, then I went back to Aldo's office with him and waited there for him to bring the file back from Records.

Aldo's office is neat, a reflection of his own personal tidiness that borders on the neurotic. I toyed with the idea of moving his stapler over two inches and his pencil holder from the left corner to the right corner of his desk just to see if he'd notice. But I knew he would. And it would probably ruin the rest of his day.

I was intent on studying a gape-mouthed bass on a plaque behind his desk, wondering why anybody would want to shellac a dead fish and nail it to a board, then hang it on a wall like it was supposed to be something pretty. Then something rustled behind me.

"Stivick," somebody barked. "Where's Stivick?"

When I turned, a chunky but well-groomed man stood in the doorway. Harland Harper.

I shrugged and gave him the old nobody-here-but-us-chickens look that usually keeps me out of trouble. Only this time it didn't work. He narrowed his eyes and pursed his thin little lips.

"What the hell are *you* doing here?" he demanded.

I straightened my shoulders. "I could ask you the same thing."

"I'm city prosecutor. I work here." He glanced around the room, then brought his brimstone eyes back to me. "What are you doing here?" he asked again.

Before I could make anything up, Aldo's head appeared behind Harper. I glanced to where his hands were. There, just past Harper's left sleeve, was the edge of a manila folder.

"Mr. Harper!" Aldo cleared his throat and somehow managed to look more obsequious than usual.

Harper spun around and glared at Aldo. "What's she doing here?" he demanded.

Aldo looked confused. He opened his mouth, then closed it. He glanced toward me, opened his mouth again, then closed it. He finally managed to say, "We had lunch."

I cringed for Aldo. Harper looked disgusted. "Do you know who she is?"

"Uh—"

"She's related to those cat burglars."

"Alleged," I said.

Harper turned and frowned at me. "What?"

"*Alleged* cat burglars, Mr. Harper. You keep forgetting. It's important."

His mouth formed a snarl. Aldo was behind him, shaking his head, mouthing the word *no* and making gestures for me to shut up. I thought Harper was going to say more, but instead he waved a chunky, manicured hand in dismissal and turned to Aldo, who dropped his frantically gesturing hands and fixed his mouth into a noncommittal straight line just in time.

"I need four more paralegals," Harper said, "and I need someplace to put them. You fix it, Stivick. I need them yesterday!"

Then he swirled out of our presence like a tsunami wave leaving distress, if not destruction, in its wake.

Aldo didn't move until the outside door slammed shut. Then he walked into the cube and set the folder on his desk. His hands were shaking.

"Whew!" He forced a weak smile. "Boy, was he upset."

I reached for the folder. "This it?"

Aldo held on and glanced nervously over his shoulder. "Uh, maybe—"

I looked up at him. "Maybe what, Aldo? Maybe I should just disappear because some people have a problem with who my parents were?"

I hadn't meant to sound so angry. I hadn't realized I *had* sounded so angry until I saw the hurt in Aldo's eyes. "I'm sorry, Aldo. I—I didn't mean that. You're trying to help me."

"That's okay, Ronnie. I don't mind."

He handed me the folder. I *shouldn't mind and* you *should*, I thought.

"There's something weird about that file," Aldo said.

I paused, hand on the cover. "What?"

"I got down to Records and found out they usually keep things for a maximum of five years. I asked them to look anyway, and there it was, on microfiche. I made a copy so you wouldn't have to go down there to see it."

"Great. Thanks, Aldo." I reached down for my backpack to stuff the folder into it, but Aldo started to fidget.

"Uh," he said.

"What?"

"Uh. Maybe you ought to read it here, Ronnie. I don't think I should let you take it with you."

"Why not?"

He launched into a long explanation that had to do with keeping his job, supplying information on the sly, and should it ever get into the wrong hands—by accident of course, because I'd never betray him, he was sure—that he would lose his job and then where would we both be?

"Right," I said.

Coaxing him out of this frame of mind could take hours and probably would cost me a dinner. With Aldo standing guard at the door in case Harland Harper showed up again, I dropped my backpack onto the floor, steeled myself, and opened the file.

48

Blackie welcomed the glass of cold Anchor Steam beer that Marcus, the barkeep, brought over to him. It was his second one of the evening and my third. It had taken me that long to get around to mentioning the file. Blackie had to raise his voice over the hum of the other people crowded into the Quarter Moon Saloon.

"So what was in there?" he asked.

"In the file?" I shrugged. "It was pretty cold and clinical, Blackie. Mostly there was just a bunch of stuff, you know, 'Passenger A this . . .' and 'Passenger B that. . . .' I just skimmed it."

I tried to act like it wasn't any big deal, but I'd almost broken down over the contents of those pages. That's why I'd quit reading after the first couple of lines. I'd skimmed until I found the page with the filled-in square for the odometer reading. I figured if I needed to, I could always go back and check the rest of it out later.

Blackie said, "So they went eleven and seven-tenths miles. Where's that take them?"

"From the garage where my mother had the oil changed, home, then over to Marcel and Henri's house is six miles."

Blackie grunted. "So you got five and seven-tenths miles up for grabs."

"Less."

I'd continued straight on Sunset and jotted down the odometer reading when I crossed Santiago. That added another three and seven-tenths miles for a total of nine and seven-tenths miles. Blackie listened, following my math and my logic.

"So you got two miles," he said.

"If I split the two in half, their destination was one mile away from the crash site." That afternoon I had pulled over and dug a map out of the old Toyota's glove box. Then I drew a free-hand curved line on the map extending from either side of Sunset and Santiago. That gave me roughly a one-mile radius from the crash site.

The rest of the evening, until I'd finally given up and met Blackie here, I'd spent going through my parents' old address book, checking addresses against the marked-up map.

When nothing panned out there, I'd waded through more pity again and tried calling the people in the book I hadn't already called before. Most were disconnected, but the half-dozen old friends who hadn't moved each said they didn't know anybody who might have lived in the area at the time.

"There is one thing, though," the last person I talked to said. Her name was Eugenia Vargas and I remembered her as a sort of Carmen Miranda–looking type—showy clothes, lots of jewelry, and always a big, big smile and a giggle for me whenever she came to the house.

"That night," she said, "no one wished to mention the trial. The day's testimony had been bad, and, well, Marcel met everyone at the door to exact a promise to not bring up the trial. Our goal was to make them forget their troubles, at least for the evening. Then your father left, alone and briefly, and when he returned, his face was unclouded. And when he spoke to Olivia, she kissed him and embraced him.

"Everyone noticed, but people were shy, they didn't want to intrude. But you know me, Veronica, I marched right up to the two of them and asked if they'd had good news. 'Cisco reached for your mother's hand and held it. 'Very good news,' he said. 'Regarding the trial perhaps?' I asked. He winked at your mother and beamed. 'Yes,' he said. 'Mr. Brady will deliver us our victory.' "

"Mr. Brady?" I asked. "Who's Mr. Brady?"

"That, my dear *niña*, I do not know. Your father did not elaborate. Minutes later they were thanking their hosts and saying good-bye. And that, *niña*, was the last time I saw them."

So I'd called everybody in the address book all over again to ask what, if anything, they knew about Mr. Brady. I started with Diego.

"Eugenia is a drunk," he said without ceremony. "She's making it up to be important."

Everybody else said basically the same thing, but less bluntly. I scoured every angle I could think of anyway without turning up a thing and in the end found myself hanging on to Stendahl's clue. It seemed the most solid angle to work.

I explained all of this to Blackie and said, "The only flaw is if they didn't go down Sunset like Stendahl said they did. But I shouldn't be too far off. My dad always took the most direct routes and he always used the big thoroughfares like Van Ness and Lombard and Sunset or Park Presidio."

Blackie snuffed out the match he'd used to light his cigarette and squinted at me through the smoke.

"Let's see the map," he said, beckoning with the fingers of his free hand. Before he looked at it, he said, "How about your friend? Harper?"

"I checked him out," I said. "He's always lived in Sea Cliff. And it just wouldn't make sense to set up a meet on a residential street at one A.M. or whenever."

I watched Blackie study the map, feeling suddenly hopeless and vaguely despondent. "Maybe Philly Post is right," I said.

Blackie's head shot up, a surprised scowl on his weathered face. A woman at the next table batted her eyelashes furiously in a bid for Blackie's attention, but he didn't seem to notice.

"Post? What's fuckin' Post got to do with this?"

"He thinks Stendahl is playing a head trip on me."

"You're not thinkin' straight, Ventana. This thing's gotcha turned around. Let me work it."

"No. I can do it."

"Suit yourself. But who you gonna believe, doll? Some asshole cop or your guts?"

I smiled. "You're right, Blackie." In my heart I believed Julius Stendahl knew something. But was that because I wanted him to know something? I thought about it, trying to clear my emotions from the facts. Ackerman. Sam Ackerman had led me to Stendahl. Ackerman had been right. And so was I.

The brunette at the next table knocked her wallet off the edge of her little table so that it landed at Blackie's feet. He glanced over, then did a double take as she leaned down to retrieve it, giving him a one-eighty view of her suddenly enhanced cleavage. Her eyes were on Blackie the whole time. Blackie winked at her, then turned back to me.

"You work this thing, you got to trust your instincts, doll. What's Post gonna tell you? You think he's goin' to jump at the chance to make what they're callin' a twenty-year-old traffic accident into a twenty-year-old open homicide?" He snorted. "Where you been, doll? What're you thinkin'? Sure he's gonna tell you it's shit."

I listened some more to Blackie's version of a pep talk, then, when he asked what I planned to do next, told him I'd thought of one more angle to work the Mr. Brady lead.

"My grandmother put all my parents' stuff in a storage locker in South City after they died. She gave me the key and told me to go through it when I was ready."

Blackie squinted at me through the smoke billowing from his mouth, but he didn't say a word.

"And then, I guess, when she died, I just took over the payments."

I picked up my bottle of Anchor Steam, but it was empty, so I set it down again. "It seemed easier, you know, than having to go through both her stuff *and* the storage locker too."

I didn't tell him that I'd gone out there a million times and only gotten as far as the door, that I'd even touched the lock but lost my nerve and simply walked away without ever going inside.

"So anyway," I said. "Maybe there's something about Mr. Brady in there."

"You want me along, doll?"

I shook my head as I waved to Marcus for another beer. "Thanks, Blackie. I'm all right."

"Your call," he said easily, then let his eyes wander to the next table and to the black-haired beauty with the cleavage.

"Hell, doll," he said, bringing his eyes back to meet mine. "I know you're all right."

49

Marina Murieta wasn't all right. She was huddled with a dark-skinned, dark-haired boy outside my apartment door when I left Blackie with his newfound love and went upstairs to go to bed. Marina looked up, bleary-eyed and dazed when she heard my footfall on the steps, and when she caught sight of my face, she burst into tears and sobbed as she pulled away from the young boy and ran toward me.

"Ronnie!" she cried.

She grabbed my waist and held on, burying her face into my shoulder, clutching me like her whole life depended on it. I put my arms around her and glanced over at the boy. His baseball cap was on backward and his pants drooped from his waist. He smiled weakly, nodded an awkward hello, then averted his eyes.

I gently peeled Marina off of me and looked

down at her mottled, green-eye-shadow-stained face.

"Hey," I said softly. "Are you okay? Are you hurt?"

She shook her head and kept on sobbing. The floorboards creaked behind one of my neighbors' doors.

"Let's go inside," I said, pulling her gently along as I unlocked my own apartment.

Inside, she collapsed onto the sofa. Her friend followed us in silence and stood timidly near the lamp, halfway between Marina and the closed door while I checked Marina for any signs of physical injury—torn clothing, bruises, scrapes. She didn't look injured, at least not physically, so I glanced at the boy and said, "Do you know what this is about?"

Marina's head jerked up. She said, "I told him not to come. I said he should stay out of it."

"Stay out of what?" I said.

Marina looked suddenly horrified all over again. She covered her splotchy face with her hands and started crying harder than she had before. The boy stayed planted between us and the door, slouched shoulders and averted eyes saying all he needed to say about the awkwardness of youth.

"What's your name?" I asked.

"Javier," he said.

As soon as he spoke, I recognized the voice I'd talked to over the phone, the one who'd been giving me the periodic "Marina's okay" updates over the past few days.

"I'm pleased to meet you, Javier. Thanks for bringing Marina to me. Do you know what this is about?"

"Marina's not feeling too good," he muttered.

"Should she go to a hospital?" I asked.

"Oh, no," he answered quickly. "Not like that."

"Okay. One of you has got to tell me what's up."

He raised his hands, palms out, and started shaking his head as he took a step backward toward the door.

I sighed. "Okay. Let's see if we can get her to talk. See if you can find a clean glass over there," I said, gesturing toward the kitchen alcove. "She could probably use a drink of water."

He moved like an athlete even though he looked pudgy. While he washed a glass from the sink, I turned back to Marina.

"Tell me about it, Marina. What's going on?"

Her sobs were down to hiccups now, the kind you get when you've had a good, long cry. The kid brought over the glass of water and handed it to her.

"Thanks, Javier," she said in a tiny voice I'd never heard before. She drank a couple of sips, then held the glass in her lap with both hands and stared down at it.

"Better?" I asked.

She nodded.

"Good. Okay, let's hear it. What's the deal?"

She exchanged a quick look with Javier, who chewed his lower lip and shook his head imperceptibly, like he was trying to get her to keep quiet about something.

"Come on, Marina. Talk to me."

"I wanted to tell you. I wanted to say something the day we followed the Fat Man, but I couldn't." Still staring down into her lap, she took in a deep breath. "You know my uncle?" she began.

"Jake?"

She nodded.

"Yes," I said, wondering how a guy who'd been dead a year could affect his niece this way.

"You know what he used to do?"

I glanced over at Javier. He was staring at Marina like he thought she was making the biggest mistake of her life.

"He used to kill people, Marina. For pay. But he's dead now. He won't ever hurt you or your aunt again."

"Do you think he was bad?"

I started to answer, then stopped. There was more to the question than what I was hearing. "What do you mean?"

"You said he was evil. You said he was bad because he killed people."

Now I was even more confused. "Marina, I—"

"I killed him," she cried. "I shot him!"

"Your uncle?"

Marina curled up in a tight little bundle, shaking her head, rocking and sobbing.

"The cop," Javier said.

I looked up, still confused. "What?"

"She's talking about the cop in the van,"

Javier said. "Only she didn't know. She didn't know he was a cop."

The blood-spattered corpse in the van. *Marina?*

She raised her eyes to meet mine, and the pain I saw in them broke my heart. Fourteen-year-old girls didn't deserve to feel such pain.

50

"He told me to meet him," Marina explained.

She'd stopped crying now, but her voice sounded hollow and weird. "He kept showing up every place I'd go, and I'm like, why's he doing this to me? He came up to me the night before and said to meet him on Twenty-second by Potrero. I got my uncle's gun, the one he had under the floor in his closet, and I—I—I shot him. I walked up to the window of the van, and there he was smiling all nasty at me, and I shot him."

I remembered Caballos's gun tucked into his van's glove box. "Did he have a gun? Did you see one?"

Marina shrugged.

"It's important, Marina."

"I don't know."

"Did he threaten you?" I asked her.

"He was going to kill me. He was kickin' me around."

"He struck you?"

"No. He was *playing* with me, messing with my head. I knew he was going to end up killing me. I *knew* it."

"Did he say so?"

"Well, yeah. I'm all, like what're you gonna do? An' he's like, what do you think? Talk to the cops, you're dead."

"And then what?"

She kept her eyes down. "I shot him."

"Tell me exactly how it happened."

"I shot him, okay? I pulled the trigger," she said angrily.

"Where was the gun?"

"In my hand."

"You were holding the gun while you were talking to him?"

"Not at first. It was in my pocket."

"All right. It was in your pocket. What did he say that made you pull it out?"

"I don't know. I can't remember."

"Did he threaten you?"

Marina glanced across at Javier. "I shut my eyes," she said softly. "I pulled the trigger. And then I ran. That's all I remember."

I thought of the sprawled-out bloody mess I'd seen in the van.

Marina bowed her head. "I hated not saying anything to you about it."

"What'd you do with the gun?"

Another quick look at Javier. "I threw it away."

"Where?"

"I don't know."

"Think you can find it?"

"Why?"

"Can you?"

Marina shrugged.

"What kind of gun was it?"

"Black."

I glanced at Javier. "Did you see it?"

Marina said, "I think my uncle called it a .357 Magnum."

"Are you sure?"

She looked at me and her eyes were like soulless empty caverns. "What's gonna happen to me now, Ronnie?"

I guess I should have called Philly Post. Or Checker or Marks. But I called a lawyer instead. And not just any lawyer. I called Diego Torre.

51

"*Preciosa!*" he cried when Marina and I walked into his office the next day. Diego Torre's gray hair glistened in the sunlight streaming through the window behind him. The effect was a halo of light around his head and stocky shoulders. Knowing Diego, he'd probably picked this particular office just so he'd be able to stand before clients and adversaries alike with the rising sun at his back, looking for all the world like God.

He worked in Embarcadero Four now, in the Financial District, a lifetime away from the little North Beach basement office he'd started out in way back when he represented my parents in their first and only trial. And he dressed the part now, too, crisply barbered, with manicured hands and those thousand dollar John Gotti suits.

"*Un abrazo,*" he insisted, extending his arms.

I left Marina behind, circled the desk, and

succumbed to his bear hug and to the rich, vaguely musty scent of pipe tobacco on his clothes.

"We meet again so soon, *mi bonita*," he said, studying my face briefly before letting go. "This is truly *un placer*."

I retraced my steps back to where Marina was waiting in front of the big desk and dropped into one of the plush chairs. Marina did the same. Diego was the last to sit. When he did, he fixed his attention on Marina and smiled.

"I do not believe we have met."

When I introduced them to each other, Diego said, "Where do you go to school, *mija*?"

Marina stared back at him, eyes sullen, lips pouting. "I'm not your *hija*," she said.

I slid my foot over and kicked her ankle.

"Well, I'm not," she insisted.

"Cool it, Marina. This guy's going to pull your butt out of the fire—maybe."

She glanced over at me. "Is he any good?"

I looked at Diego and winked. "Are you?"

He spread his arms expansively and beamed. "I am the best," he said. "Now, *dígame Marina*, do you attend Mission High?"

Marina nodded.

"Have you studied the course Civics?"

Marina pulled a face.

"Ah," Diego said. "You must not have had a teacher named Magda Torre, eh?" He turned to me. "I told you five of Magda's students last year received college scholarships to study political science."

Beside me Marina fidgeted in her seat. Diego must have picked up on her uneasiness because he smiled graciously at me and at Marina and said, "So what has your young friend done that requires the services of counsel?"

We'd convinced Javier last night that it'd be better for everybody if he went home and stayed out of things for a while. Now I wasn't sure it had been a good idea. He was a sensible boy, and good-hearted, and he'd somehow given Marina a legitimacy she, with her green luminescent eye shadow and grungy clothes, didn't have when she was just by herself.

I exchanged looks with Marina, then met Diego's questioning eyes. "You know that undercover policeman killed in the Mission District?"

Diego's face turned grave. He looked at me, then at Marina. "You have information on this crime?"

Marina stared at the floor and nodded.

"She knows who did it," I said, and cut my eyes quickly toward Marina. She didn't notice, but Diego did. He got my meaning instantly.

Nodding, he said, "I see." Then he turned to me. "And you, *mi preciosa*? You are here as her friend?"

"Yes."

"Muy bien."

His tone was matter-of-fact and businesslike at the same time, calculated to make you comfortable, to make you feel you were in good and capable hands.

"Perhaps it is best that we talk of hypotheticals? Do you know, Marina, *qué es un* hypothetical? It is like telling a story—suppose this happened, then that happened, and then something else happens. We talk about what the *circunstancias* might be and then we talk about the *consecuencias* and what the best routes to follow would be under those circumstances. *¿Comprendes?*"

Marina looked up. She was scowling. "You don't have to talk to me in Spanish. I know English."

Diego laced his fingers together and laid his hands on his desk. "Very well, then. On with our hypothetical. Let's suppose a fourteen-year-old girl has information about the death of an undercover policeman. What could that information be?"

While Diego gently quizzed Marina, I debated how much, if anything, to say about the tie-in to Julius Stendahl and my parents. Marina could connect Caballos to Ackerman, since she'd seen him dump Ackerman's body. But nobody knew Ackerman was working a story about my parents when he was killed and dumped at the site of my parents' accident—yet. Nobody except maybe his killer.

As things stood now, nobody would believe Marina. Nobody would believe a kid from the barrio was being threatened by an undercover policeman. Nobody would believe she had good reason to fear for her life unless I could prove Caballos killed Ackerman. Then maybe Marina's fears would seem credible.

There was such a thing as justifiable homicide. Or self-defense. Or something. And maybe, just maybe, if the courts showed some kind of understanding, Marina could find some sort of peace within herself and be able to live with what she had done.

I looked up and listened. A stillness had suddenly filled the room, but Marina was still talking.

Most of her tacky green eye shadow was gone now, wiped away with the tears. Huddled in the big leather office chair, she looked impossibly frail, younger than fourteen and more vulnerable than I'd ever believed possible. Her voice was a whisper, and this time her words carried the full weight of the horror of what she'd done.

"And that's when I pulled the trigger," she said. "I ran. Maybe I dropped the gun there. Maybe I threw it away someplace else. I can't remember."

My heart ached for her. She kept talking for a couple more minutes, then Diego rose from behind his desk like the interview was over. He said something, but for some reason I couldn't hear his words. I couldn't understand him. All I knew was that Marina looked horrified.

"What?" I asked him. "What did you say?"

He said Marina was going to jail.

52

I stood up quickly. "Diego, can I talk to you outside?"

He glanced at Marina. She sat quietly in her chair, expectantly. She seemed relieved.

"With your permission," Diego said to her.

Marina didn't seem to hear. She glanced over at me.

"It's okay, Ronnie," she said.

I forced a smile and touched her arm. "Don't worry. We'll get you out of this, Marina. Diego's the best."

"I don't want out. I did—" Her voice broke. "—I did something bad. I—I . . ." Her words just sort of evaporated and she looked at me with huge brown eyes that were filled with pain. "It's okay," she said again softly.

"Give us a minute," I said to her, and followed Diego out to the hall.

"She will be all right, Ronnie," Diego said before I could open my mouth.

"What do you mean? She's going to jail."

"Not jail. The Youth Authority."

"Same thing."

"Come, Ronnie. You are a parole officer."

"Not anymore."

"Ah, well. You once were. And *por supuesto*, you should know it is not so bad. Many children get the structure and discipline they need there. Regular, balanced meals, a good night's rest. Some even do better in school because they are not allowed to skip classes." He smiled. "You know these things."

Diego was right. I'd seen a lot of kids turn around after a few months of attention and structure in the Youth Authority system. But Marina wasn't a bad kid. And how would they treat her if they thought she'd killed a policeman?

"I know what you are thinking," Diego said. "She will be fine. I will assure you with my *reputación*."

Three hours later we were leaving the Hall of Justice and Marina Murieta was staying behind. They were taking her to Juvie as soon as the van got there. Marina's aunt had just left in a flurry of neighbors, relatives, and tears, and Diego and I were crossing the big marble entryway downstairs, making our own way to the exit.

"Did you have to let her confess?"

Diego glanced over at me, I guess to let me know my tone was a little sharp. I didn't care; I was annoyed he hadn't done more.

"No," he said. "I did not. But your friend, she

is a strong-willed young lady. Almost as strong-willed as you. As your mother. And there are some things an attorney cannot prevent. I advised Marina against doing so. I advised her in the strongest of terms, several times."

I sighed, and as I stepped through the big glass doors, I was surprised to see the sun still shining. It was just past noon. "Well, what happens next?"

"I will see her in the morning. We will talk again."

He started down the steps and I followed.

"Diego?"

He stopped and turned to look at me. His eyes were tired. He seemed suddenly old, and I realized with a start that my father would have looked this old, too, if he'd lived. "Yes?"

"I need to talk to you about . . . something else."

"*Seguro, bonita.*" He checked his watch. "I have time. Come, let's find a café."

He took my elbow and steered me down the street, past a couple of cheap diners and into an artsy café that seemed more North Beach than Hall of Justice. We both ordered double espressos.

"Now, *preciosa*," he said as the waitress served our coffee. "You wish to speak to me about something else, yes? And I have given some thought to our last conversation. Now that you are a private detective, perhaps you will consider from time to time helping an old friend out by doing some work for my firm."

"Diego, wait—I'm working something right now. And as a matter of fact I could use *your* help."

"Of course, *preciosa*. I forgot. You wished to ask my advice. Who is your client?"

"Me."

"You? But—"

"I'm looking into the accident, Diego."

"The accident?" He pretended not to understand. "But—"

"You told me you didn't go to Marcel's party that night?"

He hesitated, then said, "That is right, *mija*. I was in the middle of a trial."

"Did my parents know anybody who lived near Marcel? Say, within a mile?"

His eyes filled with sympathy and confusion. "But *¿por que?* If it was an accident . . . ?"

"There maybe was a witness."

Diego sat up, surprised. "*No puede ser.* This cannot be. Who? Why has he been silent all these years?"

I told him about meeting Julius Stendahl.

"No, *mija*, no. This is not true. This man is lying. *Tiene que ser un loco.* To begin with, your mother was devoted to 'Cisco. As 'Cisco was to her. She would never have looked at another man. And if this *loco* had seen what he now claims to have seen, surely he would have come forward. Please do not let this lunatic cause you further grief, Ronnie. Now, put this old history aside. Say you will investigate my case for me."

"My mom never mentioned him?"

"*Nunca.* Never. This man is obviously troubled. He is using you for whatever obscure reasons he has. Now, please, leave all this behind. The pain is too great to relive, *no*? Now, *mija*, with your permission, I will finish *mi cafecito* and we will speak of other things."

I watched him sip the coffee from the tiny espresso cup and remembered him as he was twenty years ago: a bright, dark-haired young man full of life and vitality. He still had that energy, but it was smoother now, more directed. He'd been, back then, as my father said a million times, like family.

"Tell me about the trial."

He set his cup down and stared gravely out the window. The second wave of workers on their lunch hour was spilling onto the sidewalk. I watched them and waited.

"It is painful for me, *mija*. All this talk of the past is very painful. I have friends—many friends—I always have. But never have I found one to be as good a friend to me as your father. To contemplate the past again like this is to open a deep wound."

"Yes."

Our eyes met. I held his gaze until he finally gave in. "You are just like your mother," he said, and sighed. "What is it you wish to know?"

I searched around inside my head, not sure what I wanted to know. I'd hoped he'd just start talking and something would click, but he was asking for direction. "What happened the last day at the trial?"

He shrugged. "Nothing significant. Harper had just finished examining the diamond expert."

"And what came out of that?"

"Nothing. As far as I'm concerned, Harper was—what is the term?—grandstanding, making a show for the jurors by having the expert explain how diamonds are cut and set and how they can be easily transferred from one setting to another. It was utter nonsense and I objected several times, but the judge overruled me each time."

"Did he examine anybody else that day?"

Diego thought a minute. "There was talk of bringing out the informant."

The state's case was based on the word of a prominent jeweler—Diego called him the informant—who'd been arrested and said my father had tried to sell him pieces of jewelry that had been missing from the then-mayor's home for about a year.

"And what happened?"

"Harper said he wouldn't be ready until the next day, so we adjourned."

"What did my parents do?"

"We all went back to my office to review the day and plan for the next. That consumed an hour or so. I remember we were brief because Olivia said they were going to a party that night and they wanted to spend time beforehand with you."

And as it turned out, I wasn't home when they got there. So my mom left me the note. "Was that the last time you spoke to them?"

He blinked, then looked out the window again.

"Diego?"

He stared down at his empty cup. " 'Cisco called me later that night, about an hour or two before the accident, around midnight. I was at my office. He sounded happy and said he had a surprise for me."

"And he didn't he mention a Mr. Brady?" I'd asked him once already, but felt like I needed to ask again.

Diego shook his head. "When I asked, he said it would be a birthday present for me. The next day—the day they died—is my birthday. Then he invited me to fly down to Acapulco the next week to go deep-sea fishing. I reminded him we were in the middle of the trial and he said of course, but that it would all be over by then."

"Is that how you had it figured? If things had progressed the way you saw them progressing, would the trial have been over in a week?"

Diego looked troubled. I could tell he didn't want to answer. Finally he said, "I thought it would have taken a little longer, only because . . . the prosecution tended to want to include everything even remotely related to the case and the judge was allowing them to do so."

"Do you think my father knew something?"

"What could he know?" Diego shook his head sadly. "Your father, he was always optimistic, remember?"

"What aren't you telling me, Diego?"

He reached his stubby, manicured hand across the table and took mine. "Please, Ronnie," he said. "This man who is telling you these things, he is *un loco*. Spare yourself the pain. It was an *accidente*."

53

The red light on my answering machine was flashing when I got home. I dumped the box I'd lugged upstairs onto the table and rushed to rewind the tape. I was eager for some kind of distraction, anything really, because I felt so crummy.

I'd finally gone down to the storage locker in South City, the one with my parents' stuff in it, but I didn't get far, mostly because of my grandmother. She'd left a note taped to the top of the first musty box just inside the door. The note was addressed to me and it said that she hoped one day I'd be strong enough to read this piece of my parents' history, that when I found the box I'd be ready.

I'd stood in the doorway of the storage locker staring down at the yellowed slip of paper in my hand for a long time before I realized my fingers were trembling. *What's to be scared about?* I asked myself. *This is what I wanted*, exactly *what I wanted*.

But something held me back, something about the irrevocability of a message from the dead. I reached out and touched the edge of the box. *Do it.* I hesitated, then tore off the tape and spread open the top. There were papers inside, mountains and mountains of papers, documenting, word for word, in transcript form, my parents' trial.

Now, in my apartment, as the phone-message tape played back, I stared at the big box. I'd read through it all, every word, sitting on the cold cement floor of the storage building: testimony from the Burglary Unit detective, from the burglary victims, the fingerprint expert, the jewelry expert, the fence, the guy who claimed to have heard, between the arrest and the arraignment, my dad's admission of guilt.

All of it, every single word, was damning. The case seemed so solid that I didn't even want to think about it.

The answering machine clicked off. I looked up as it whirred into automatic rewind and realized I hadn't heard a word. I punched Playback again, and held my breath as I listened to the young man's voice on the tape.

"This is Javier, Ronnie. Marina's friend. She said to call you an' tell you I got something important. It's something . . . well, it's important."

I jotted down his address. Then instead of grabbing my keys, I reset the machine and sat for a minute staring at the box of transcripts. I was thinking, thinking about the trial and about how much my parents and their well-intentioned friends, and even my dear, sweet *abuela*, had sheltered me from everything having to do with the trial. I reached for the phone and called Diego Torre.

"*¡Querida!* What a surprise."

"You were going to lose, weren't you?" I said.

"Lose what?"

"The trial, Diego. I just read the transcript."

There was dead silence on the other end.

"The case against my parents was a slam dunk for Harper. You'd have to be from Mars not to see that. They were going to go to jail, weren't they, Diego?"

He sighed gently into the silence, then said, "Why, *mija*? Who—How?"

I told him about the storage locker and my grandmother's note.

"*Ay, mija.* I wish . . . I wish I could have spared you this . . . this anguish."

"They were going to jail, weren't they?"

"That is something we will never know."

"How can you *say* that! The jewel expert I.D.'ed the jewelry. The guy who shared a cell with my dad before the arraignment told everybody how my dad said he'd done it. The woman said she saw both my parents go into the building. It's all pretty overwhelming, Diego."

He sighed again.

I said, "They were going to jail, weren't they?"

"*Preciosa*, please."

"Come on, Diego. What did you have that was even remotely exonerating?"

"They were going to testify."

"Do you expect me to buy that? Hearing them wouldn't have put a dent in what Harland Harper had. What aren't you telling me?"

After another long silence, in a voice so soft it was almost a whisper, he said, "There were rumors, Ronnie, after *el accidente*, rumors that 'Cisco and Olivia were distressed."

What did he mean? I closed my eyes and waited. Something dark and heavy twisted inside me. I couldn't think. I couldn't feel. I couldn't understand what he was saying. When he spoke again, his voice was still gentle.

"They were distressed, *mi querida*, about the possible outcome. But these were only rumors."

"What?" I tried to see through the fog that was filling my head. "What are you saying, Diego?"

"Please do not press me."

"I need to know, Diego. You *have* to tell me. I don't understand what you're saying."

I waited him out, and after a few interminable seconds of roaring silence, he said, "I speak only because you insist. There were people, some said they were so distressed that perhaps the *accidente* was not in fact an *accidente*."

I stared at the cardboard box and saw my sweet mother's face, smiling, full of warmth and love. When she told me they would never leave me, I never once doubted her.

"That's not true," I heard myself saying. My voice was high and pinched. "They wouldn't have. You know they wouldn't, Diego. How were you going to defend them in court?"

"Ronnie. Veronica. Please—*don't.*"

"Did you even *have* a defense?" I shouted. "They put their trust in you. They were counting on you."

Diego refused to say anything more except how sorry he was that I was so upset and that I needed to lay the whole thing to rest, it'd been twenty years after all. So I took a couple more jabs at him, then hung up and went to the fridge for a beer.

Diego was wrong. They wouldn't have taken their own lives. And they wouldn't have left me. They just wouldn't have.

I slumped onto the couch and stared at the wall. If there'd been rumors about suicide, why hadn't I heard them? Sure, I was just a kid then, but I would have known. Kids pick up more than adults give them credit for. And no way were my parents suicidal. Diego as much as disproved it when he said my father intended to go down to Mexico for deep-sea fishing the next week.

I finished the beer and was about to walk out the door just to put some distance between me and the whole thing, especially the box of transcripts, when the phone rang.

"Is this Ronnie?" The small young voice on the other end was hesitant, but I thought I recognized Marina's friend.

"Javier?"

"Yes. Marina said to call you. I have it here. I found it an' I told her I found it an' should I throw it away, but she said call you an' do whatever you say to do."

"What did you find, Javier?"

"The gun, man. Want me to throw it away? I know someplace nobody'll find it. I can do it now."

"No. Wait! Don't. Take it—no. Where are you? I'll come get it."

When I got there, I saw that he'd wrapped it in a tattered rag and put it inside a shoe box that smelled faintly of foot powder.

"Where did you find it?" I asked.

He shrugged.

"How do you know it's Marina's uncle's gun?"

"It is," he said, then fixed his huge brown eyes on mine. "Are you going to throw it away? I got a place—"

"No, Javier. We have to turn this over to Diego."

"I thought you were her friend."

"I am."

"But for sure she won't get off. What kind of friend are you?"

"Marina turned herself in because she feels bad about what she did. She wants to do the right thing. Hiding this gun isn't going to make things any better."

"It's less evidence," he said logically.

I stared at the heavy box in my hands. "I know."

Diego wasn't happy to see the gun either, but in his calm, pragmatic way, he didn't seem to think it was the end of the world. And neither one of us mentioned my call.

"We don't have to turn. it over," he said, addressing the issue at hand. "We must return it to the place Javier found it and pray the investigators do not discover it themselves."

"Is that legal?"

He nodded and handed the rag-wrapped shoe box back to me without opening it. "It will be best to handle it this way. Give it back to the boy and tell him to place it exactly where he found it. Poor child, she has already confessed. Perhaps this gun will make no difference. Perhaps it will. The poor child was simply defending herself. If they find the weapon, we may simply stipulate to the shooting. No jury will convict."

But when I went to see Marina during her noon visiting hour to tell her the good news, she had a feverish glow in her eyes, like a martyr's.

I listened while she protested and insisted we turn in the gun. She told me she had faith—in God and, if not in the system, then in justice. If she was punished, she said, maybe she could live with what she'd done. Yes, she knew she'd been scared and, yes, he probably would have killed her, but if she had known how awful it was going to feel to take a life, she would have let him kill her.

"My uncle made it seem so easy," she said softly. "But you were right, Ronnie. Turn the gun in. *Please*. I won't feel right unless you do."

"I'm not going to do that, Marina. You need

to go with what Diego says. He knows the rules and you need to play by the rules and—"

"And try to get off? I don't *want* to get off. I did something bad."

"Fine," I said. "If you want to tell the police where to find it, go ahead. I gave it back to Javier and told him to put it in the exact spot where he found it. So tell them. But I won't. And Diego won't."

"Fine!" she shouted. "I will."

We glared at each other, jaws clenched and hearts pounding, until I finally said, "Please, Marina. Don't. Don't do this."

Tears welled up in her eyes. "I have to," she whispered, holding back a sob. "Can't you see? I have to."

54

I'd just slipped the key into my building's front door when I heard a car honk on the street behind me. It was a full-bodied honk, vintage voice of Detroit, and the sound lifted my spirits.

A sparkling but old green Cadillac waited by the line of parked cars along Grant Avenue. Its passenger-side window was rolled down, framing the driver's head as he leaned across the seat and peered out at me.

"Miss Ventana!"

It was Reece Cunningham, the wheezing old newspaper reporter, yellow tobacco-stained teeth bared in a smile, beckoning to me with a claw-like hand.

I slipped my keys into my pocket and crossed the sidewalk.

"Get in, Miss Ventana," he said, glancing over his shoulder at the short line of cars behind him. "I got something to say, you want to hear it."

The car took off like a rocket as soon as I pulled the door shut.

"Street this narrow ought to be closed," he said, reaching for a stubby, unlit cigar lying in the pulled-out ashtray. He stuck it between his teeth, then glanced sideways at me. "You okay, Miz Ventana? Pardon me for asking, but you look like you just lost your best friend."

"I'm okay, Mr. Cunningham. Thanks."

The car's tan leather seats were worn smooth and comfortable. And the thing was huge. He had about as much space in the car as I had in my studio apartment. It was like riding around on a couch with wheels.

We turned left onto Union, then headed past Washington Square Park toward the Presidio before he said, "I'm busy and you're busy, so I'll dispense with the formalities and get right to the point, if that's all right with you, Miss Ventana."

I told him that was fine, but could I ask him something first.

"Of course, Miz Ventana. Anything. What's your pleasure?"

"Did my parents ever mention a Mr. Brady to you?"

"Can't say they did. In what context?"

"The trial."

He pondered it a moment, then chomped his cigar and shook his head. "Can't say that they did."

So I asked what he'd wanted to talk to me about.

"I'm concerned about young Sam Ackerman's

death. I know it was linked to his story, but I'm too old to work it." He glanced across at me. "How do you feel about the coppers? Same as your mom and dad did?"

"What do you mean?"

"I mean your father didn't trust them worth a spittoon, Miss Ventana. Maybe less. And Olivia, well, she was too much of a lady to say so, but you knew where she stood, and it wasn't on the blue side of the line."

I smiled. "What do you have, Mr. Cunningham?"

"I didn't tell Ackerman this and I didn't tell you before, either, 'cause I just remembered this morning. That night, the night your parents died, I went to the scene. There was a lady out there running around in a bathrobe. Nobody was paying attention to her, but she just wouldn't go away. She was an iddy-biddy thing, couldn't have been over five foot, and soft-spoken so you could barely hear her. I suppose that's why the coppers didn't bother with her an' I suppose that's why I should have. I didn't, though. I can't even tell you her name." He smiled apologetically. "All I can say is, maybe she saw something."

55

I spent the rest of the day feeling depressed about Marina and walking door-to-door up and down Sunset Boulevard, checking to see if anybody listed on the page I'd copied out of the reverse directory from twenty years ago was still in the neighborhood. I found three families, but nobody remembered anything about April 24th. Then, late in the afternoon, I knocked on a door almost a whole block down from the light post.

A shriveled but spry old man with a lined, pale face opened the door. He looked dressed for a garden party: white dress shirt tucked into an alligator belt that matched his shoes, silk tie, linen slacks, and a matching vest. The sparse ivory-colored hair on his head was combed tidily back with some kind of sweet-smelling pomade.

"Hello, young lady." He smiled, and his eyes disappeared behind a blanket of wrinkles. "What can I do for you this afternoon?"

"Are you—?" I glanced at the list in my hand. "Mr. Simmons?"

"That's me." He waited expectantly, politely, sort of like a waiter at a nice, old-fashioned restaurant.

"My name's Ronnie Ventana," I said, launching into my rote introduction. "I'm looking into an incident that happened down the street a long time ago. Did you happen to live there twenty years ago?"

He beamed. "I can do better than that. My parents and I have owned this house for seventy-five years. I've lived here all my life."

"Do you remember a car accident that happened down the block at Santiago? It was twenty years ago on April twenty-fourth."

He smiled. "The cat burglars. Of course."

"You remember?"

"How could I forget? It was the only thing Mother talked about for months. She saw it, you know."

"She *saw* the accident?"

"Oh, yes," he said, warming to the topic. "She saw everything. Father was mortified. Here it was three—or was it two? in the morning and Mother was out there in her robe and slippers, chattering away to anybody who'd listen. Dad finally called our doctor and had her sedated. Otherwise I think she'd still be out there. Poor Mother, she'd never had that much excitement in her life. Well, really, none of us had." He stopped and studied me closely. "Did you say you're a reporter?"

I handed him my card.

"A private investigator. And—oh, my!" He glanced up quickly. "Are you related to the cat burglars?"

"Did you happen to see the accident, Mr. Simmons?"

"Oh, no. I was in bed sound asleep. So was Dad. Mother was the only one who saw anything."

"Is she home? Would it be possible to speak to her?"

"Speak to Mother? About the accident? I'm sure she'd love nothing greater."

I peered over his shoulder. "Is she home?"

"I'm afraid not. But wait here and I'll get my jacket. We'll go to her."

I followed Henry Simmons north across town as he drove his vintage Plymouth at a dignified motorcade speed of eighteen miles an hour. At the Knolls Home for the Elderly on Laguna, a perky blond receptionist greeted him by name and smiled at me.

"This is Ronnie Ventana," Simmons told her.

"How are you today, Ms. Ventana?" she asked.

"Remember the Ventana cat burglars?" Simmons said. "The jewel thieves? She's the daughter."

The woman's smile froze.

"That's wonderful," she said. "Is Miss Ventana here to visit your mother?"

"Yes. Ms. Ventana is a private investigator and she's—"

"It's this way, isn't it?" I said, taking his

elbow and guiding him toward the only doorway leading from the foyer into the body of the building.

"Straight ahead," the receptionist called after us. "It's the last door on your right."

"She must be in the garden," Simmons said.

There were two old men in one corner of the garden playing checkers and a bunch of Miss Marpleish–looking gray-haired women chattering and playing bridge at a table by the door. The solo people were scattered around the back of the garden, each a respectful distance from the other, some drowsing, some just sitting and staring at nothing, but everybody in the sun.

We found Mrs. Simmons alone on a lawn chair next to a rosebush, reading. She was a tiny woman with hair as white as her son's and his same penchant for dressing well. Her hair was combed neatly in a chignon and she was wearing a perfectly pressed navy-and-white print blouse with a navy skirt and matching navy pumps.

"Henry, dear. What a surprise!" Her voice was low and throaty and full of life, like somebody's half her age. Simmons bent down and kissed her cheek, then motioned toward me with barely suppressed excitement.

"Mother, this is Ronnie *Ventana*—she's the cat burglars' daughter."

Mrs. Simmons set her book aside and smiled up at me. "How lovely to meet you," she said. It was almost like she was expecting me.

Henry gathered a couple more lawn chairs

and we sat down. "About the accident," I began. "Your son tells me you saw it."

"I couldn't sleep that night. I'd just had a cup of hot milk and I was warm, so I decided to open the front door and get some air—back then we had a screen on the front door. In any event I'd just stepped onto the porch and I heard a big roar. I looked across the grassy patch, you know, up Sunset, and there they were, racing down the street."

"They?"

"Yes, dear. Your parents in their little gray sports car. And someone else driving a black Lincoln Continental."

56

My chair nearly tipped over. Above the crashing roar of my pounding heart, I said, "There was another car?"

Mrs. Simmons's soft blue eyes filled with concern. "Why, yes, dear. Didn't you know? They both must have been going sixty or seventy miles an hour—maybe faster. They just flew by. It looked as though they were racing each other, you know, seeing who could go the fastest." She glanced at Henry. "What do they call those, dear?"

"Drag racing?" he said.

"Of course. And of course the sports car was ahead, but only by a bit. I had no idea what it was all about, but I ran out to the yard. This may sound strange, but it looked from my perspective as though the Lincoln forced the little car into the median. It was only a split second, then it was all over. I saw flames shooting out of the sports car."

And screams? I wanted to ask as my blood ran cold. *Did they suffer or did they go quietly?*

"Miss Ventana? Are you all right, dear? Henry, bring Miss Ventana a glass of water."

I blinked, and saw her kindly face.

"No, that's okay. I'm fine."

Henry sat back down, but not before looking at his mother for permission first.

To me she said, "I'm so sorry, Miss Ventana. I'm not being very sensitive, am I?"

"What about the Lincoln, Mrs. Simmons?"

"It vanished. But another car drove up and stopped. A young man was driving. It was another dark car, perhaps—perhaps a Ford. I started toward him—I don't know why—I should have gone back to the house and called for an ambulance, but I suppose I was too flustered to be thinking quite right. When he saw me, he sped away."

"If I showed you a picture, would you recognize him?"

"Absolutely. He was pale and his face was round."

Julius Stendahl.

"He looked shaken—positively shaken."

"Did you actually see the Lincoln force my parents' car into the pole?"

"That's how it appeared. It was a hideous thing to see. Simply hideous."

"How about the license plate number or anything that might help identify the driver or the car?"

"Nothing. But while I was out there, the

black Lincoln drove by again, going in the opposite direction. It slowed at the accident and I
noticed the front fender was scratched and bent
along the side. I believe he—"

"It was a man?"

She nodded.

"What did he look like?"

"I don't know. I can't remember. I just
remember seeing the scratch on the fender."

"Was he alone?"

"Yes. I tried to get the police to go after him,
but no one would listen." She twisted her frail
hands in her lap and sat quietly, but I got the
impression she had more to say. I waited and
finally she spoke.

"There's something else I should tell you,
Miss Ventana. I haven't told this to anybody, not
even Henry Senior. When the car crashed, I ran
down there and stood—and this is something I'll
be ashamed of as long as I live—I stood fifty feet
away staring at that car, but I couldn't make
myself go any closer. I was *afraid*. I wasn't
thinking straight. I'm sorry, Miss Ventana. I truly
am. The ambulance crew said they both died
instantly, so there was nothing I could have done,
but at the same time, I didn't know that. I've felt
so ashamed all these years. If they'd been alive, I
might have been able to make a difference by
going up to the car. And I didn't."

Henry stirred. "Oh, Mother, don't be so melo-
dramatic. They were dead. It wouldn't have made
any difference at all. Why don't you just forget
that part of it?"

"Maybe you'll be able to make a difference now," I said.

Mrs. Simmons frowned. "How?"

"Would you be willing to tell the police what you've just told me?"

"If you think it will help. But you know, dear, I already have."

57

I stared at the photocopied accident report in my hand. The first time Aldo Stivick had let me look at it, I'd skimmed it. I hadn't been able to read it at all. But now that I knew what to look for, here it was in black and white:

Subject Lena Simmons states she believes a black Lincoln Continental forced victims' vehicle into light pole.

"Ronnie?"

I looked up. Aldo had his coat on and he was standing by his office door. "I've got to lock up, Ronnie," he said. "I have a flute lesson at six o'clock."

"Right."

I folded the paper in fourths, then started to put it into my back pocket.

"Uh, Ronnie?"

"What?"

"Uh, I don't think that's such a good idea. I think you'd better leave that here."

I glanced at the folded sheet in my hand. "This? The report?"

"Uh-um . . . Remember we talked about it last time and decided it wouldn't be a good idea?"

"Oh, right. I forgot," I said, unfolding the page, then slapping it into the folder and laying the folder on top of a bunch of other identical folders in Aldo's In-box. "I guess I don't really need it. I'll come back later and look at it if I have to, okay? You're in a hurry."

I stood and grabbed my backpack off the floor, then swung it and knocked Aldo's pencil cup over. "Oh! Sorry! Let me—"

"No, no. I'll do it." Aldo rushed forward and started picking the pens up off the floor. I slipped the report out of the folder and into my backpack.

"I guess I'd better go," I said from the door.

Aldo was so engrossed in making sure he was putting the pencil cup in the exact spot it'd been before, that he didn't even look up when I left.

My getaway would have been a clean one except that when the elevator doors opened for me to get on, Philly Post was inside, clutching Javier's shoe box. I couldn't help but stare—at the box.

"Get in," Post barked, jamming his thumb down on the Door Open button.

"Oh, uh, that's okay," I said, stepping back and waving my hands in front of me. "Go ahead. I'll—I'll catch it on the way down."

"Get in, Ventana."

I didn't budge, so he stepped off the elevator and put his face right up in mine. "You knew about the gun," he said.

I swallowed and backed up another step. "What gun?"

"Come off it, Ventana. You're not foolin' anybody. I'm telling you so next time you come around begging for some special favor, you'll know why I turn you down."

"Don't be so petty," I said, then slid around him and lunged into the elevator milliseconds before the doors slid shut.

Downstairs I hit the pay phones and called the personnel number for the police department. They were closed, so I dialed the Taraval Station, the station that would have handled an accident on Sunset. When a deep male voice answered, I asked for Officer Kent Dugan.

"Dugan? Hold on. Anybody ever heard of a Kent Dugan here?" A pause. "We got no Dugan here."

I called the other nine stations with the same result. Then I did what I should have done in the first place, I looked for Kent Dugan in the white pages. He was there, with an address in the Sunset.

He lived a couple of blocks from the zoo on Vicente near Forty-second in a modest single-story house over a garage. It was painted a light green color that looked drab in the fog.

A stout, thick-necked man with thinning red hair and a red cardigan sweater answered the door. His feet were in scuffed-up, fleece-lined moccasins, and a TV blared nonsense in the background. He looked like he had just woken up.

"Are you Kent Dugan?"

He seemed to wake up a little bit, but his expression stayed neutral. "Who wants to know?"

"My name's Ronnie Ventana. Are you the Kent Dugan who used to be a police officer?"

"Ventana?" Now he was definitely awake. "Are you—?"

"That's right. Did you write this?" I handed him Aldo's copy of the accident report.

He glanced at the signature, the printed name, and the badge number at the bottom of the page and said, "Where'd you get this?"

"A friend."

He stared at the page and shook his head. "That was a long time ago," he said, handing it back. "Why are you asking about this now?"

I held the sheet up and pointed to the middle of the report. "Do you remember this woman?"

He glanced down and squinted. "Lena Simmons?" He shrugged. "Like I said, it was a long time ago."

"Maybe these will refresh your memory."

I pulled out the black-and-white photographs of the accident Reece Cunningham had given me. Dugan studied the first one, then flipped quickly through the other two and handed them back.

"It was a mess," he said without emotion, then looked me in the eye and waited.

"Did anybody follow up on Mrs. Simmons's statement?"

"I followed procedure. I asked around."

"And?"

"Nobody else saw anything."

"So you dropped it?"

"Corroboration." His expression softened a little. "Look, Ms. Ventana, I don't know why you're asking around about this now, but for what it's worth, I can tell you this lady was full of beans."

"What do you mean?"

"She was a citizen, right? The biggest excitement she's seen is when her cake goes for two bucks at the school bake sale."

"I'm afraid I don't follow. Why would that make her unreliable or inaccurate?"

"I was a cop for eight years. Sometimes people get excited, they forget themselves. I'm saying they get carried away and sometimes they get confused."

"And how did Mrs. Simmons get carried away?"

Kent Dugan leaned up against the doorframe and shoved his hands deep into his pants pockets. He came across as a patient man, maybe not too bright, but even-tempered. I wondered why he'd stopped being a policeman.

"Mrs. Simmons said she saw a black car force the Beemer sport into the pole, right? I take her statement and tell her she can go, but what's she do? She hangs around the scene in her bathrobe and slippers getting in everybody's way. Then the D.A. drives up—I guess somebody called him 'cause he was handling the trial and all—and this lady says that's the car that did it."

"Harland Harper's?"

He nodded, the expression on his face telling me how crazy he thought it was.

"Was the front fender scratched?"

"What?"

"The D.A.'s front fender—was it scratched?"

"Not really." He shrugged. "There was some nicks on it. No big deal. His son had trouble getting out of the garage with it or something."

"Is that what he told you?"

"I don't remember exactly, but whatever he said was consistent with what I saw. It didn't look even close to anything you'd get forcing somebody off the road like that." He watched me for a moment. "Look, he said he'd been home all night with his wife."

"Did you interview her? Did anybody compare the paint on his bent fender with the paint off my parents' car?"

Kent Dugan pulled his hands out of his pockets and stared at me like he thought I was nuts. "Do you know what you're saying? You can't be serious. Do you honestly think Harland Harper killed your parents?"

"I don't know, Mr. Dugan. But if he did, I'm going to find out."

58

Helga Harper was a delicate, fine-boned woman with wispy blond hair, empty eyes, and expensive taste in jewelry. My parents might not have liked her—but at least they would have enjoyed browsing her safe deposit box and talking carats.

Her apartment wasn't far from mine, and parking is hell on Telegraph Hill, so I walked. She was on a tiny street called Edgardo Place with a splendid bridge-to-bridge view and lots of space. The view alone made her rent worth about a hundred times more than mine.

"I'm sorry," she said, ushering me into a lushly furnished living room with skylights and a solid glass wall that framed the Bay. "I don't quite understand why you want to see me. I've been divorced from Harland for years. We talk now and then, but we never see each other anymore."

She walked to one side of the room and

slipped behind a bar, then offered to mix me a drink.

"No, thanks."

"Hope you don't mind if I do." She put together a martini that looked strong enough to cure anything but what ailed her, then strolled elegantly to the white sofa that faced the Bay and gestured for me to sit. I did, then watched her float down into a matching white chair. I got the impression the martini in her hand wasn't her first one of the day.

"Now," she said, settling into her chair and smiling a practiced society smile. "Tell me what you'd like to hear regarding my dear, darling Harland."

She sipped delicately at her martini, closing her eyes when she drank, like it was the elixir of the gods. For her it probably was.

I looked around the room for family pictures, but there weren't any. "Do you and Mr. Harper have a son?"

"A son? No. Why?"

"Do you remember my parents' trial?"

"How could I forget? Harland was obsessed with that stupid case. Forgive me, but he couldn't talk about anything else for months. That trial was going to be his ticket to the mayor's office. It was going to make him the somebody he thought he was born to be. To tell you the truth, I just tuned him out after the first few weeks. My lawyer served him with the divorce papers right about then, and all Harland cared about was talking me into waiting until the trial was over.

He wanted to blame it—the divorce—on the pressures of the trial."

"That wasn't true?'

Helga Harper lowered her eyelids suggestively and said, "The only pressure on Harland was the pressure every night between him and his little prostitute."

"He was having an affair?"

She smiled. "How civil of you to put it that way. She was a prostitute and he was her regular customer. I wouldn't call that an affair."

"Do you know her name?"

"Angelica something—Molson, Morton, something like that—I never really wanted to know. Harland bought her a house, a little love nest where he spent most of his time."

"Did he put the title in her name?"

"It sure as hell wasn't in his. My divorce attorney told me we couldn't touch it when we were splitting things up."

"The night my parents died, Mr. Harper said he was with you."

"I know."

"Was he?"

She met my gaze without flinching. "Back then Harland only came home to change clothes. And to talk about that stupid trial. I guess his prostitute was too dumb to know what he was talking about. At least I understood enough to nod in the right places."

"Do you know where he was that night?"

"I know he wasn't with me."

I forced my voice to stay neutral, nonjudgmental, when what I really wanted to do was scream at her. "Why did you say he was?"

"He promised me a bigger settlement if I did."

"Why are you telling me this now?"

"It was twenty years ago. Who cares?"

"There's no statute of limitation for murder."

"Murder? How nice," she said, draining the last of her martini and offering me the practiced smile again. "For you, I mean—not for Harland."

"Do you think your husband—"

"*Ex*-husband, please."

"Do you think your ex-husband is capable of murder?"

"Let me put it this way: If something or somebody came between him and what he wanted, I don't think he would hesitate."

"But he was winning the case," I said.

She rose and took her empty glass to the bar for a refill. "Are you sure you won't join me?" she asked, lifting her glass. "I've been told I mix the best martini in town."

"No, thanks. Listen, Mrs. Harper, did he ever mention anything to you about the case being in jeopardy? Can you remember him saying anything like that? That he might lose?"

"Why is everybody so suddenly interested in that night?" she asked, resuming her seat in the overstuffed chair across from mine.

I sat up. "Who else have you talked to about it?"

"That reporter."

"You talked to Sam Ackerman?"

"That's right. Ackerman. He called."

"What did you tell him?"

"Nothing. He never showed up."

"But when he talked to you—over the phone, I mean—what did he say?"

"That he wanted to talk to me. He didn't say why. He didn't even mention my ex-husband."

"Then how do you know he wanted to talk about the accident?"

She frowned and looked puzzled. "I don't know. That's a good question. Maybe Harland . . ."

"I thought you didn't have any contact with him now."

"I don't. But he called the other day to chat." She shook her head. "I don't really know. *Somebody* must have told me."

"You talked to your husband—I mean ex-husband? He knew about Sam Ackerman's call?"

By now the second martini was half gone. "I'm sure I mentioned it. He—Yes, I did. He seemed . . . interested." She looked amused. "You don't think Harland killed your parents, do you?"

"I don't know who killed them, Mrs. Harper, but if it was your husband, he's going to go to jail."

Her martini sloshed over the rim of the glass and dribbled onto the expensive white fabric of the chair. Helga Harper brushed at the damp spot with a sloppy gesture, then smiled.

"Oh, goodie."

59

"Here it is, Blackie."

Blackie has just come back from a cigarette break on the steps of City Hall. We'd rolled through what seemed like miles of microfilmed city records, and he'd been ready to give up, but I'd talked him into taking a break instead. I breathed in the pungent smell of tobacco smoke that clung to his clothes as he leaned in close to read the screen.

I said, "Angelica Merton, see?"

But my heart sank as I read further. Angelica Merton had owned a condo twenty years ago, not a house, and the address was way out on Balboa which put it out of the radius I needed. "It needs to be by the great Highway, Lake Merced or around Stern Grove," I said.

"Tough break, doll." Blackie surveyed the room, then looked down at me. I knew he was going to suggest leaving.

"Do me a favor," I said, cutting him off before

he could speak. "Check over in the marriage records."

"For?"

"For Helga Harper's maiden name."

While Blackie vanished, I rolled through the property records for Harland Harper. None of the buildings listed was even remotely close to where I needed them to be.

Blackie popped back a couple of minutes later. "Gunterson."

I whirred through and located Gunterson, then ran through all the property in her name, checking it against the city map I'd brought with me. She owned a lot of cheap condos off of Caesar Chavez, some in Opera Plaza and a couple of houses.

"I got a hit, Blackie! This is it," I said when the last document whirred up to the screen and I checked my map. "See? This address—it's two blocks from Lake Merced."

Blackie pulled up the empty chair next to mine and sat down with a scowl. "He was winning the fuckin' case, doll."

"I know, I know."

That was the stickler: motive. It didn't make sense. My parents were his ticket out of oblivion. Why murder them? I looked into Blackie's grizzled face and said, "There's got to be some kind of explanation."

"Yeah?"

The way he said it, flat and without a molecule of enthusiasm, you'd think I was trying to talk him into a root canal. I tapped Helga

Gunterson Harper's name on the blue-screened console in front of me and grinned to try to pump him up.

"I know you like women, Blackie. And beer. But how to you feel about martinis?"

60

The plan was for Blackie to coax whatever details I hadn't out of Helga Harper in hopes of uncovering a motive. She seemed like at one point in her life she preferred the upscale type, but maybe Blackie could talk her into trying the working man for a change. He'd done it before.

For my part, I drove straight to the garage my mother took her car to that last day. I set the odometer and drove to the little cottage we'd lived in when they died, then went on to Marcel and Henri's former house, then to Helga Harper's rental property by Lake Merced.

According to the city records, she didn't own it anymore, but I pulled over at the modest, single-story house and stared at it. It wasn't unusual. The roof was shingled and the window frames small, made out of cheap aluminum. The house didn't stand out from its neighbors. There was nothing special about the last place my parents had visited.

I sat in my car and stared at the house until one of the neighbors came out and asked me what I was doing. He was a stiff old man with roughened, gnarly hands and a kind face. His clothes were clean but worn: dungarees, scuffed-up work boots, and a zippered jacket.

"Have you lived here long?" I asked him.

"Bought that house for my wife thirty years ago," he said, his chest puffing up with pride as he pointed at the house next door. "Made the last house payment when I retired in January."

He couldn't tell me anything much about the Harper house except that it'd been rental property until a "young couple" bought it. The couple's kids were in college now, he said, so maybe they weren't so young anymore and maybe it'd been longer than he thought. And now that he thought about it, they'd moved in twenty years ago.

I thanked him and drove straight up Sunset to Santiago, then pulled over again and checked the odometer. It read eleven and seven-tenths miles. Exactly.

61

I staked out the Hall of Justice and waited. Two hours and a zillion quarters in the meter later, Harland Harper charged down the front steps. He had a briefcase in his hand and he looked like he was in a hurry. So was I.

I caught up with him before he reached the end of the block.

"Mr. Harper," I said. "Wait up."

When he turned and saw it was me who'd flagged him, his expression went from impatience, maybe mild annoyance, to outrage.

"You!" he bellowed, flushing with anger. "What do you want?"

"I know you met with my parents the night they died," I said. "You lured them to your ex-wife's rental properly at Lake Merced. I know you followed them and you ran them into that light pole."

He stared at me, stone-faced, for what seemed like a solid minute. Then he threw his head back and snorted. "That's preposterous."

"Is it?"

"You don't know what you're talking about."

"You owned the house they went to. It was in your wife's name, but you owned it. You met them there, then you followed them and you killed them."

"This is outrageous! It's ludicrous. *Why?*" he asked, and he sounded genuinely puzzled. "What possible reason would I have for murdering your parents? For murdering *anyone?*"

"Because they—Because you—" I stopped and looked into his unfeeling eyes. My parents had seen the cruelty in those very eyes and they'd seen more, something else, and they'd paid the price.

"You, young lady, are unstable," Harper said, then leaned in close. "You'll never prove it because it didn't happen." Then, with another derisive snort, he turned on his heel and went off in the same direction he'd been headed before I'd stopped him.

I stood there on the sidewalk feeling empty and defeated. *Why? Why would he kill them?*

I tried to will my parents back, at least in spirit, to lead me to an answer, to point me in the right direction. But they wouldn't come. And for the life of me, I couldn't figure it out alone.

62

I turned around to head back to the car and saw Philly Post fifteen feet away in the middle of the sidewalk staring at me with an unpleasant look on his face.

"Great move, Ventana," he said, strolling easily toward me. "You tryin' to alienate the whole world or just anybody who talks to you?"

"Save your insults, Post." I barged past him. "I've got nothing to say."

"Hey, wait a minute. I want to talk to you."

"Make an appointment."

He caught up with me and fell into stride beside me. "Real funny, Ventana. I heard what you said to Harper. You don't really think he killed your parents, do you?"

"No, Post. I was just indulging myself in some good-natured teasing with the man who prosecuted my parents."

"Come on. You can't really—"

"I do. And so did Sam Ackerman. That's the story he was working. It's what got him killed."

"By Harper, right?"

"By Pedro Rubio, alias Herbie Caballos, alias Arnaldo Contreras."

"Rubio was a cop."

"A dirty cop, Post. And Harland Harper is dirty too."

"You're not thinking this through. He— Harper's got an alibi for—"

I stopped. "You checked him out?"

Post shrugged. If I didn't know better, I would have thought he was embarrassed.

"Then you know his alibi's no good," I said. "I talked to his wife this morning and she says he wasn't with her."

"She sign a statement?"

"No."

"You get it on tape?"

"No. Why?"

"I just came from there. She told me he was with her all night from nine o'clock on."

"She's lying."

"Could be."

"He got to her."

"If that's how you want to see it, go ahead. You need to start looking at somebody else, Ventana. Harper's got no opportunity and no motive. As far as I can see, all he's got is your goat."

I started walking again and Post came after me. "Forget about him. I want to talk to you about the gun."

"What gun?" I said, then my heart sank a split second later when I remembered Marina.

"The gun the kid turned in. There's a problem with it."

"Oh?"

"It's the wrong gun."

I stopped again and looked into his unreadable face. "What are you saying?"

He studied me, then said, a little bit surprised, "You didn't know."

"Of course I didn't know. Now, what are you talking about?"

"The bullet that killed Officer Rubio came from a nine-millimeter—a Glock. She gave us a three-fifty-seven."

I smiled. "That's great! That's terrific. Have you released her?"

"We still got the confession."

"But if the gun—"

"We don't know about that gun. She's the only one saying it's the one she used. She could have set us up for it in a bid to get us to let her walk." Post hesitated. "Talk to her, will you?"

"And say what?"

"See if you can convince her to give up the right gun."

"She did, Post."

He bent his bushy head down close to mine. "This kid's dickin' us around like she's been doin' to her teachers, she's gonna be looking at some major regret here."

His words clouded my confidence in Marina for a second. Post saw me waver. "Talk to her. Tell her to turn in the right gun."

"*You* talk to her, Post. *You're* the one who wants her in jail."

63

When I got back to my car, the last person I wanted or expected to see in the parking lot was Cocky Burnett. But there he was, eager and present.

"Yo, Ms. Ventana! You ready for me to set this thing up yet? I got yer guy on the string. He's sittin' there with the fat bucks just waitin' for us. Talkin' large, man! That's real good, you know. Most times all's I get is spare change. But this one's big, right? What you got is *real* big. 'Cause that's what I told him."

"Cocky, I—"

"You're not gonna pull out on me, are ya? I put a lot into this, Ms. Ventana. I got some other very important ventures I neglected on account of this thing you're sayin'. Ya gotta come across on this, Ms. Ventana. You got somethin' this hot, you can't just sit on it, ya know?"

"Forget it, Cocky."

His face fell. "You went with somebody else."

"I don't have anything, Cocky. I just wanted to know how it works, that's all."

Cocky sort of shrank back and raised his hands waist level, palms out. Grinning, he said, "Oh, no, Ms. Ventana. I can't give you names."

"I didn't ask for any."

"It don't work that way. I'm not saying you'd cut me out of nothin', but a fella's gotta protect himself. Otherwise he's outta business for good."

I reached for the car door and opened it. "Go away, Cocky."

"But I got Mr. Big. It's all set up. All's I need is for you to say when. But it's gotta be soon, 'cause this guy's gonna sit on the string wit' nothin' for just so long, ya know. I got 'im, but he's not gonna wait around forever."

"I guess he's going to have to," I said, then got behind the wheel.

"Wait." Cocky stepped forward and stood in the way so I couldn't close the car door. "I gotta talk to you."

"I don't have time for this, Cocky."

His face turned dark and desperate. "But—but—there's somethin' else. I gotta do this with you, Ms. Ventana. I gotta do it or I got nothin'."

"That's not going to float with me, Cocky. I'm not buying this. Now, will you get out of the way so I can close my door and leave?"

"But listen. This D.A.'s pulled out on me now. He's givin' me a hard time and says I can't testify now on account of this Brady-crap thing."

My hand froze on the ignition. "Brady? Who's Brady?"

Cocky scowled. He was glad to have my attention, but seemed upset I wasn't focusing on what he'd wanted me to. "Not who—what."

"Well, then, what?"

"It's the end of my meal ticket, that's what. Unless you help me out and—"

"Why? What is it?"

He was about to launch into his plea for help again, then seemed to give up. "It's some legal case says anything the D.A. gets that helps the other side has to get turned over."

"Like what?"

"Like me. They say I got undermined credibility on account I got a habit. I got busted and they took care of it all, an' now they're sayin' government witnesses can't do dope. They knew all along—that's how I got into this. So listen, Ms. Ventana, you got something and I connect you up and get a piece, okay? I'm just gonna be the middleman, is all. You gotta testify yourself 'cause I can't any more."

64

t felt odd to be in the parole office and not be working there. I'd been gone six years, but nothing had changed—the same dank brown walls, the same stale air filled with echoes of desperation and lies and disappointments.

"His name's Arthur Pensk," I told Edna. She'd been the one who'd convinced me to stay the extra year past when I should have left public service. She thought I was good at supervising the cons, but nobody else but the cons agreed with her.

"Here," she said, yanking a thick folder out of an interoffice mail envelope. Then she said, "Tell me again why this guy's so important I had to get his file out of storage?"

"His testimony was the most damning at my parents' trial. Without the confession my dad was supposed to have made in jail, they didn't really have a case."

"Okay. So what are we looking for?"

"Something incriminating. Something that could be considered bad enough to make a jury doubt his word."

"Like what?"

She laid the file on a table by the window and we both sat down.

"I don't know," I answered, then flipped the soft manila folder open and prayed I'd know it when I saw it.

"Still doesn't get you anything," Post said, sucking on the last remnant of a peeled orange. The citrus zest in the air made his drab office seem less dreary. "If the ex-wife can alibi him, if he was physically someplace else, giving him ten reasons why he'd want to bump off your folks doesn't get you anything."

"But Arthur Pensk flunked three consecutive drug tests. And he was Harper's main witness." I'd shown Post the memo the head of the Parole Board had sent to Harper telling him so.

"Just putting a copy of a letter in a file doesn't prove you sent it or the guy you sent it to got it, much less read it. You need to read your P.I. manual again, Ventana."

"Why don't you want this killer caught?"

"You got no proof he is a killer. Look at it the way a judge and jury would. Just 'cause I'd like to see your buddy Coogan get hanged doesn't mean I'd do it. Same goes for Harper and your folks."

"You're not listening, Post. Harper was using the case to launch his career, to set himself apart. He wasn't going to let anything get in his way.

But then he got caught. At the very least he was going to look foolish and lose the case. And realistically it would probably have been worse. He probably would have been charged with prosecutorial misconduct, maybe disbarred. When my parents showed him they knew what he hadn't turned over, he flipped. I know my dad would have given him an out, a gracious exit. My dad wasn't the kind of guy who had to rub your nose in it. But Harper went crazy. He followed them and he killed them."

Post's voice oozed patience when he spoke. "Only he didn't flip, or kill them, or murder innocent reporters around the world, because his wife says he was with her that night."

"She's lying."

He shoved the memo I'd given him back across his desk toward me. "It's been twenty years, Ventana. The trail is cold. Let 'em rest in peace."

65

By the time Blackie caught up with me at the Quarter Moon Saloon, I was on my second cup of coffee. I'd spent all afternoon drowning in Anchor Steams, trying to figure out a way to nail Harper. The brilliant plan I'd come up with had seemed brilliant through the amber prism of beer, but I needed to look at it with a clear head to know if it would really work.

Blackie slouched into the chair beside mine and signaled Marcus for a beer, then grinned at the empties lined up on the table. "Looks like I got some catchin' up to do, doll."

"No, you don't, Blackie. Did you talk to her?"

"The Harper dame? Sure. She oughta patent those martinis."

"Did she—"

"No dice. She's not comin' down off coverin' for him. Fucker musta promised her the moon."

Marcus set Blackie up with a beer, poured another shot of coffee into my cup, and was back behind the bar before we'd even noticed he'd left it.

"I've got an idea," I said.

Blackie gulped some beer and kept his expression neutral. "Yeah?"

I glanced at my watch, then reached for the front section of the *Chronicle* at my feet. "He's speaking tonight," I said. "At the Press Club."

"Harper?"

I nodded and Blackie waited, sexy blue eyes squinting with curiosity. Finally he said, "I know you don't want to hear the fucker talk."

I grinned. "I had something else in mind, Blackie. Something a little more private. And productive."

99

Sea Cliff abuts the Pacific and Lincoln Park on one side and the Presidio and the Avenues on the other. It's got mansions and lawns and views across the wide water that sometimes let you see as far as the Farallones. Most of the time you can't, though. Fog coats the world in Sea Cliff and keeps everything in a soft, cool gray glow that muffles sound and makes you feel like you're in some kind of cold heaven.

Since my shabby '77 Toyota would have stood out like a cactus in Sea Cliff, and so would Blackie's old Buick, I'd borrowed my friend Sady's catering truck. Somehow the moisture from the dense fog seemed to bring out food odors inside the van. It smelled like we were driving a vat of pressed garlic around town.

As I slowed at the curb on Scenic Drive, Blackie pulled his head in from the open window and asked, "Where's the hit?"

"Down there." I pointed to an off-white

darkened mansion with a tile roof, a perfectly manicured but small front lawn, and a gated trellis on one side that led to the backyard. Harland Harper's home.

I left the keys in the ignition, grabbed my black backpack full of tools, and took a deep breath. "Let's do it," I said.

We made a big show of ringing the doorbell and waiting, in case anybody was watching, then discreetly headed for the back.

The flimsy latch on the trellis gate wouldn't have kept a butterfly out. And once I started working the lock on the sliding glass door in back, I fought back my disappointment. "He doesn't have a burglar alarm," I whispered.

"Good," Blackie said, then stepped back and looked at the second story. "You want down or up?"

"Up," I said. Up is always trickier. And I figured my bones were more resilient than Blackie's if anything went weird and somebody needed to jump out a second story.

The lock clicked easily. I slid the door open and stepped inside onto a slick terrazzo tile floor dotted here and there with glossy, angular Italian furniture. If I was giving points for interior design, I'd have to ding Harper big time—the quirky furniture clashed with the lush richness of the ornate trim and moldings and the general opulence of the place. And the terrazzo tile floor just made things worse.

"What're we lookin' for, doll?" Blackie asked

as we made our way in the dark toward the front of the house.

"Check ledgers, bank statements—anything we can use to track him buying off his ex-wife. Oh, and if you see a copy of that parole-office letter I showed you from twenty years ago, let me know."

"Keep dreamin', doll," Blackie said, then darted across the darkened living room. He lifted a painting off the wall and set it on the floor, exposing a small, metal safe. "How about I take a look here?"

"Show-off."

He rubbed his hands together, then ran the tips of his fingers up and down the rough fabric of his denim jacket. After a moment he started working the combination dial.

"Remember," I said, "no trails, no signs of entry."

"Gotcha," he agreed, then sighed with satisfaction as the door to the safe sprang open.

"Anything?" I asked, crossing the room to peer over his shoulder.

His tiny penlight showed a short stack of folders in an otherwise empty safe. The top five had addresses scrawled across the front and held receipts and a ledger of expenditures for maintenance—painting, plumbing, landscaping.

"Rental property," Blackie said, then pawed through the rest of the stuff. It was basically legal papers—his will and some kind of trust—and a big stack of stock certificates that must have been worth a fortune.

"I'm going upstairs," I said, and left Blackie carefully placing the stuff back in the safe.

Three of the four bedrooms upstairs seemed unused—no clothes in the closets or dressers and a thin layer of dust on everything. They were impersonal to the point of motel bland, complete with cheap pastel-framed prints on the walls, tacky bedspreads, and phone books and telephones on a desk.

When I opened the door to the fourth bedroom, it looked like a hurricane had hit it. Clothes and socks and shoes were strewn everywhere, and for a minute I thought somebody had already tossed the place. But after a second look I noticed the underwear was more or less piled in one spot, the crumpled shirts in another, and the shoes in another. Mr. Harper, for all his meticulous grooming, was a slob.

The air in the room smelled musty with an underlying hint of some sickeningly sweet-scented aftershave. Or maybe it was deodorant. Whatever, combined with the stuffy smell, it gave my stomach a turn.

I held my breath and tiptoed my way through the trash on the floor to check out the mahogany bedside table. The shallow drawer held a box of aspirin, three foil packets of condoms, a couple of nudie pinup postcards, and a pint of cheap whiskey.

I stuck my gloved hand into the drawer and felt around inside the back end, then pulled it out and checked the drawer's underside. Nothing.

The digital clock on the table top said 9:37.

We'd been inside the house for four minutes. That meant we had five more minutes, seven max, before passing into the danger zone, time-wise. The more time you spend inside, the more likely it is you'll get caught. The ideal time is three minutes, but I'd need a platoon of burglars to do a house this big in that short a time.

I flashed my penlight around the room, then searched quickly through the closet and under the bed.

"Okay, mister," I muttered. "Where are you hiding it?" Whatever "it" was.

I made my way to the bathroom and peeked inside. At least the dirty towels were piled in the corner instead of strewn everywhere like the stuff in the bedroom. I poked at the pile with the toe of my shoe. Nothing. Nothing interesting in the medicine cabinet either. Nothing in the linen closet or the shower. I was about to walk out, when by instinct I reached over and lifted the lid off the toilet tank.

When I looked inside, I almost missed it. The bundle was about the size of a small book, black, and it could have been mistaken for part of the inside tank mechanism if you looked quickly. In the weak beam of my penlight it looked like it was wrapped in heavy black plastic. I plunged my arm down into the cold water and pulled it out. The bundle was hard and heavy in my hand.

"Whatcha got?"

I jumped and nearly dropped the thing, then whirled around. "Blackie! Jesus!"

He grunted and sort of shrugged. "I got jack

downstairs." His eyes went back to the package in my hand. "Whataya think?"

I pressed and probed quickly with my fingers. "It's a gun," I said, tearing at the tape binding the plastic. When I finally got it unwrapped, Blackie said, "Glock."

My heart started to race. Glocks are nine millimeters. "This could be our break, Blackie."

I dumped the plastic on the pile of towels, checked to make sure the thing was loaded, and headed for the unused bedroom farthest from Harper's. Blackie followed. At the door, before going in, I stopped.

"Get me the phone books out of those two spare rooms," I said.

By the time Blackie came back, I'd already pulled a towel out of the bathroom cabinet and was soaking that room's phone book in the sink. When he brought in the other two, I set the first phone book in the tub and stuck the other two in the sink, letting the water run so they'd soak up as much as their pages could hold. When they were completely waterlogged, I stacked them on top of the first phone book, then wrapped a towel around the gun's nozzle and fired it into the phone books.

"He won't miss a towel," I told Blackie after I'd dug the spent bullet out of the Yellow Pages and tucked it safely inside my pocket.

"I got it covered, doll," he said, moving quickly to wipe up the floor and bundle up the phone books with the towel.

I took the gun back, wrapped it up again, and

tucked it back into the toilet tank. Blackie was at the door, clutching the sodden telephone books under one arm.

"We're gone, right?"

I touched the spent bullet in my pocket to reassure myself that I really did have it, then grinned. "Right."

67

Cocky Burnett slid into the Toyota's passenger seat grinning so broadly I thought he'd split his face. "Post likes that bullet," he announced. "He likes it a lot."

"Did it match?"

"Wouldn't say. But he sure wanted to find out where I got it."

"You didn't tell him it was from me, did you?"

"You said don't say, so I didn't say. He even threatened to lock me up, but I didn't give no ground, Ms. Ventana. I ain't no amateur here."

"Did you give him the envelope?"

Cocky's smile faded.

"The envelope, Cocky?"

"Uh, yeah. Sure. I gave it to him."

"You didn't make him pay for it, did you?"

Cocky squirmed and laid a hand protectively over his breast pocket. "Maybe I asked for a couple of bucks."

"Cocky, we agreed you wouldn't ask for money."

"It wasn't nothin' to break the bank or nothin'. I need to make a livin', ya know." He tossed his close-cropped head and said, "He paid up, so what's the beef?"

"The beef is—never mind. You're confidential, right?"

"C.I. Number Four-eight-seven-five," he said proudly. "Confidential Informant. I been thinkin'. This is the way around that Brady thing, you know. I just go in confidential and nobody needs to know nothing about me. An' Lieutenant Post says confidentials don't testify, so I figure if there's any real money in the deal, it don't get strung out over time like the other way." Cocky Burnett nodded, satisfied. "Yeah, I like the way this C.I. deal works. I think I'm doin' business like this from here on out."

Cocky was pleased, but however brilliant I thought I'd been in using him, I figured it wouldn't take Philly Post long to tie Cocky to me. But I didn't care. So long as he moved on the thing, I didn't care.

I wrangled the catering truck from Sady again, parked it down the block from Harper's house, and waited. It was five o'clock when the first unmarked car pulled up. Philly Post was inside and so was a federal-looking guy. Post stepped out, glanced at Harper's house, then looked down the street and noticed the catering van.

I was in the back part of the van, peeking out

through a dark curtain behind the driver's seat, so I knew he couldn't see me, but he came over to the van and knocked at the driver's-side door just the same.

"Ventana!" he called out. "I know you're in there. Open the door."

I stayed where I was.

"I've got a slim-jim in my car, Ventana. Don't make me go get it."

He was quiet for a moment, then he said, "I released the Murieta kid, Ventana. She's cleared."

I waited a couple of seconds, then stuck my head out from behind the curtain and acted surprised. "Post! What are you doing here?"

"Cut the act, Ventana. I'm doing you a courtesy here."

"You released Marina?"

"Right. Kid's a tough sell. Wouldn't buy that she was such a bad shot. Couldn't get her to go home until I showed her the hole in the roof of the van her bullet made and the one in the side from the Glock. Even insisted on seeing the two bullets. She's worse'n you."

"But you let her go."

"First time ever had to throw somebody *out* of jail." He nodded toward Harper's mansion. "You want a front seat on this?"

"Why?" I frowned, not bothering to hide my suspicion.

He looked away. " 'Cause just maybe you could be right."

"Of course I'm right, Post. Why do I have to move mountains to make you see that?"

"This thing pans out, I figure you got a marker from me." He paused, looking more ominous than ever. "And if it doesn't, I want you right beside me."

"I promise you, Post, on my parents' grave, he's your man."

Just then Harper's Lexus pulled up in front of his house. He jumped out, shouting and gesticulating like a madman, demanding to know what was going on.

"Wait here," Post said, and crossed the street.

I waited until he'd reached Harper, then followed, but by the time I'd crossed the street, they'd moved up the walk to the front door. Harper was still shouting, threatening Post with everything from demotion to beheading.

Post seemed impervious to all the bluster. He handed Harper a folded sheet of paper, which I assumed was the warrant, then said in the same tone you'd use to ask somebody to pass the salt, "Will you unlock your door, Mr. Harper, or do we break it down?"

"I'll have your ass, Post! Your career is over."

Post waved to one of the guys in uniform, who stepped up and put a lock punch up to the door. Harper lunged for the cop, but three more uniformed cops jumped all over Harper and held him back while the other guy punched the lock out of the door.

"Upstairs!" Post shouted to the small army of uniforms and plainclothesmen charging through the now-open door.

Harper's eyes widened. He sputtered curses

and waved his thick arms in useless protest. Then he went quiet. I followed his gaze and saw Post standing in the doorway, clutching the gun, its dripping black plastic ripped partially open.

Harper's jaw dropped. Post glanced past him to look at me. If he was excited or pleased, he didn't show it. "Keep your fingers crossed, Ventana."

At the sound of my name, Harper's head jerked around. He saw me and something inside him seemed to snap. His nostrils flared. His eyes bulged. Then he broke free from the cops who'd been restraining him and ran for the trellised gates and into the backyard. I bolted past the stunned cops and ran after him, then heard them bustling behind me.

Harper was running, running through to the end of the yard, to the cliff at the end of the yard. Beyond was the yawning blue maw of the Pacific. He ran to the edge of the yard, then lurched to a stop and wheeled around to face me.

"Stop!" he shouted. "Stop or I'll jump!"

I pulled up short on the grass about ten feet away from him. I was close enough to hear the rasping sound of his labored breath, to see the deep lines in his flushed face, and to smell his fear. His chest heaved. He seemed spent, broken. The backs of his heels just kissed the edge of the cliff behind him.

From somewhere back by the house Post shouted, "Ventana! Back off!"

I locked eyes with Harper and held my

ground. "Jump," I heard myself say. "Jump, you lousy bastard."

Harper looked surprised, then wounded. "You've got it all wrong," he said, then his eyes darted past my shoulder. He shouted, "Stop! Stop or I'll jump."

"Ventana. Back off." It was Philly Post again. He sounded farther away than I'd thought he was, so I glanced over my shoulder and saw him standing in front of the pack of about ten cops clustered near the trellised gate. "We can handle this, Ventana. Now, back off."

"Leave us alone, Post."

"Ventana!"

I kept my eyes on Harper and gestured to Post to go away. "This is between me and him, Post."

Harper's breathing was still labored. His hair had strayed forward across his broad forehead in three thick greasy strands and his face glowed with sweat. He was watching me, waiting, and there was something feral and frightened in his eyes.

"You're going to tell me what happened that night, Harper. You're going to tell me—"

"You're crazy. You don't—" He gazed imploringly past my shoulder. "Get her out of here, Post. She's crazy. She doesn't know what she's talking about. She—"

"Why'd you run, Harper? Why'd you run when you saw the gun? If you're so innocent, what are you doing here on the edge of a cliff threatening to jump? Only a guilty man runs, Harper."

His eyes rolled wildly. He licked his lips. "They were guilty," he said quickly, quietly so that I was the only one to hear. "Can't you understand that?"

"You set them up!" I shouted. "You set them up so you could get ahead."

His words rushed out. "They were guilty. I had no reason to kill them. I was prosecuting them. Why would I kill them?"

"Brady," I said. "You had exculpatory evidence. Your key witness wasn't any good. That's why my parents met with you that night. They told you they knew. They probably offered you the chance to bring it out yourself instead of being exposed. But you refused, didn't you?"

He winced.

"You turned them down and then you killed them."

"You don't have any proof. I don't know what you're talking about. That was twenty years ago."

"Don't pretend you don't know, Harper. You knew exactly what you were doing. You knew exactly what you had planned when you turned them down. Hasn't your conscience ever bothered you? Don't you have trouble living with yourself, knowing what you've done?"

He stared back at me with eyes that were quickly losing their luster and their hope. "They were guilty," he repeated, but there was less conviction in his voice this time.

"Then why did you kill them?"

"I didn't—"

"What about Sam Ackerman? Was he guilty too?"

Harper ran his tongue over his small lips. He looked like he was about to say something, then just lowered his head and shook it.

"What about Caballos? What was he guilty of? Following orders? You killed them. You killed them all. And if I can't get you for my parents, Harper, at least you're going to rot in jail for Caballos and Ackerman. You're going away for that, but in my heart and in your heart, we'll both know you're doing the time for killing my parents. That gun's going to match, Harper. We both already know that. You're stuck. You're dead. So why don't you jump, you lousy piece of sleaze?"

I stood there watching him, wishing in my heart, praying, that he would jump, that he'd land on the sharpest rock down there and that he would suffer as much as my parents had, as much as I had.

"Jump," I whispered through clenched teeth. I batted something off my cheek and my fingers came away wet. I touched my face again and realized I was crying. Tears were streaming down my cheeks. I wiped at them angrily, then took a step toward him. "Jump, you bastard."

"Ventana! Hold it right there!"

Harper looked imploringly past me. "She's going to push me," he shouted. "She's crazy. Get her away!"

"I'm not crazy, Harper. Just angry." I took another step toward him and he recoiled, teetering on the edge of the rock where he perched.

"Jump," I whispered again. "I want to see you jump. I want to see your bones broken in a million pieces on those craggy rocks down there. I—"

"Ventana!" Post shouted. "Don't do this. You've got ten witnesses here. Think it through."

I lowered my voice. "Tell me, Harper. Tell me the truth. They can't hear. You killed them, didn't you?"

"No."

"Say it, Harper. Tell me. I need to hear it from you."

The cold and easy wind off the Pacific swept over me. I felt suddenly and perfectly serene, perfectly in control.

I took another small step closer and said, "It's just between you and me, Harper. If I say anything, it'll be my word against yours and you know you'll win. Say it, Harper, for your own sake as much as for mine, *say it*. Say it so we can both be at peace."

His chest was still heaving. He grimaced and blinked rapidly a few times. Then he looked past me, at the cops, swallowed, and glanced up at the darkening sky. He cleared his throat and looked down at his feet.

"You did it, didn't you? You killed them. Admit it."

"Yes," he finally said in a voice so soft that I barely heard. "I forced them into that pole."

I stood before him, stunned, as a huge roar filled my ears. He bent over double and covered his face with his hands, and for a split second I saw my parents' car go up in flames. I felt the full force of the yearning ache that for twenty years had been as natural and integral a part of me as my limbs or my vision.

Then my shoulders sagged and a huge weight lifted from me. I stared at Harland Harper until he finally felt my eyes on him. He looked up and I held his gaze, watching his expression go dead.

I'd thought his admission would make everything right. The weight was gone, yes, but I'd expected his pain to make me happy. I'd thought it would give me joy. But all I felt was a deeper sadness, and a stronger yearning for the comfort of my mother's kiss and my father's embrace, the comfort I had lost as a child and would never have again. There was no consolation for that.

I turned away slowly, deflated, but somehow oddly at peace for the first time in twenty years.

"Don't!" Philly Post shouted, and came charging toward me. But he wasn't looking at me—he was looking past me.

I wheeled around in time to see Harper lurch toward the cliff's edge. I lunged for him and grabbed his legs as he went over. I felt myself sliding with him, carried forward by the weight and momentum of his body. Then something landed on top of me and knocked the wind from my chest. An arm reached past mine and grabbed Harper's legs.

We stopped sliding. In seconds I was surrounded by heaving and grunting men, all grabbing and pulling at me and at Harper, dragging us back from the precipice.

Once we were far enough from the cliff to be safe, Post rolled off me and onto the ground beside me. He lay there scowling and panting. "Jesus," he said.

I filled my lungs with the cold ocean air and watched as the cops lifted Harper up off the ground. He looked small and ruined, a shallow, broken shell of the man he'd seemed. I wanted to feel pleasure. Everything I'd ever believed in told me I would have been pleased to see him destroyed. But all I could think was how small and pathetic this man was to try to build up himself and his career on the lives of my parents, to take down two brave and noble souls so that he could steal their fame.

I rose and followed them out to the street, to the squad car that would take him away to the jail where he'd sent so many others. He paused at the open door of the police car and sought me out with his eyes. If he wanted forgiveness, he was looking in the wrong place.

I walked up to him and looked into his ravaged face.

"You should have jumped," I said. Then I turned and walked away into the night.